Ma

to

My Heart

Stand by me

by
Grace True

First paperback edition November

Book design by Publishing Push

ISBNs
Paperback: 978-1-80227-863-7
eBook: 978-1-80227-864-4

Dedication

Praise, glory and thanksgiving to a loving Father
who makes music to my heart.
He loves me!

I give thanks to the Lord for
my angels: Lawrence and Ophelia,
my parents: Iulia and Dan,
and for a special friend that brings joy,
love and grace in my heart.

Psalm 57:7
My heart is steadfast, O God,
my heart is steadfast!
I will sing and make melody!

1 John 4:7
Beloved, let us love one another,
for love is from God,
and whoever loves
has been born of God and knows God.

May the Lord bless you and strengthen you and
guide you
as you walk on a path of love,
and may you hear music in your heart.
You are loved!

Contents

Chapter 1

The Green Bell Hospital

It was evening and the lights of the town were switching on. It was another day gone. For me, it was a bit different; I was out of my normal, safe zone. I heard music deep inside, and it sounded so peaceful. It was music in my heart. Someone was playing or singing, I was not sure which, but there was other music deep down in my heart. I wished I could stay in that place forever. It felt like home. I was loved by the Lord.

I knew it, but I also felt it. His love was not only in my heart but was covering me and made me feel like flying.

Matthew 11:28-30
Come to me, all who labor and are heavy laden, and I will give you rest. Take my yoke upon you, and learn from me, for I am gentle and lowly in heart, and you will find rest for your souls. For my yoke is easy, and my burden is light.

It was almost dark and I noticed a strange smell around me. Then I recognized the smell and opened my eyes. Where was I?

Then I remembered: earlier in the day, I had been involved in a car crash. Yes, my car was hit by a red car. That is all I could remember before it all went dark. I woke up here. Yes, it seemed familiar.

Yes, of course. It was the Green Bell Hospital, the largest in the town and the busiest, for sure.

I did not want to be in a hospital, at least not here. Why not? Well, I was a senior nurse and this is where I worked; it was "my" hospital. It was my job, my calling, my life, looking after patients daily.

This was Unit C where the ambulances brought the majority of patients involved in accidents. High-risk cases, emergencies, day and night, non-stop.

I loved looking after people and being here. My work was my life and everything I had, in a way.

My friend Laura told me that I spent more time at the hospital than at home and the hospital was becoming my new home.

She was probably right. I did feel at home here and took every opportunity to be here, doing extra shifts if needed.

I pressed the bell, and a few minutes later, a nurse came by.

"Hey, Hannah! How are you feeling, girl?"

"I'm fine, but I need to go to the bathroom, please."

"All right, I'll get you there slowly. Let's see how you can walk." The nurse kept talking. "We were all sad when we heard that you'd ended up here. Well, you know what I mean, as a patient. Maybe now you will get a chance to rest for a few days as you work way too much!"

It was hard to walk but harder to be stuck in bed. I managed a few steps with support. It was not as bad as I thought, but still, I was in a lot of pain. At least I was surrounded by familiar faces.

The long night passed and I could not fall asleep.

It was an interesting feeling to lie in bed and be taken care of. I had a few bruises, and my left hand was in a bandage.

I started to pray in the darkness and my heart grew wings. My courage built up, and I was sure things would be better in the morning. My Lord always looked after me. From all the years of walking with my Lord, I knew that. And my life had not been an easy one!

But I knew that if I rested and let the Lord look after me, carry me, He would do a better job than me. His wisdom and the revelation of His will would bring joy to my heart and soul; they would refresh me and lead me on paths of righteousness.

***

It was dark, and my thoughts went back to a few years ago. At that time, I had been working as a nurse for several years and had just been promoted to senior nurse. Things were getting better for me and my life was moving in the right direction. John always told me I was a bright, beautiful girl and constantly encouraged me.

Without his help, I would probably have been lost in the system. He was a loving, protective man and the only one I could trust in my life. He worked hard and always looked after me. He was my big brother, 10 years older than me, and he was my only family. I guess life brought us close to each other and we were always there for each other.

The phone rang and, sleepily, I picked it up. When I answered, I heard a voice speaking quickly.

"Hannah, this is Dr Parson. Get yourself here as quickly as you can. Your brother John has been brought in and is not looking good."

With my heart racing, I put some clothes on and was at the hospital in 20 minutes.

Dr Parson was just coming out of John's room.

"Hannah, glad you are here! He is not good. He is not good." He kept repeating it and put his hand on my shoulder. I looked into his eyes, trying to find some hope or encouragement, but I did not.

"What happened?"

"He was in a bad car crash. We had to do CPR and he is back, but he is not responding much."

"Can I see him, please? Let me in." Dr Parson closed his eyes and for a moment did not say anything.

"Maybe it is best that you don't go in, Hannah. Not now!"

I insisted as I wanted to see my brother, so he gave in and said gently, "All right, girl. If that is what you want. Go in."

As I went in, I felt a pain in my chest. It was such a sad sight: John lying there with blood everywhere. I could see that his pulse was weak and four nurses were looking after him.

No one said anything when they saw me. I felt so helpless as I could not do anything. Tears were running down my face and I could not stop them. I went up to him and took him by the hand. I touched his face and kept telling him it would be alright.

Suddenly, I heard him saying something and he opened his eyes.

"Hannah, my lovely Hannah. My sister!" he whispered. "I will go to my Lord... Hannah, keep going. I love you, angel!" At that moment, he tried to smile, and everything stopped. His heart stopped beating and everything went to zero. He was gone. He went to heaven to be with the Lord; the Lord had saved him and taken him to a better place.

The emergency bell rang and Dr Parson rushed in. They tried to bring him back but nothing happened. They tried so many times, but I knew he had gone.

"One day," he often used to tell me, "I will be with my only true, loving Father and I will meet Mum there too. You will see. And we will all be happy there. God is good. You will see, Hannah, God is always good!"

After 15 minutes, everyone left the room. Dr Parson looked at me and touched my shoulder.

"Hannah, we should go."

"No, I want five more minutes, please. I want to be with him."

He looked at me and was not sure whether to let me stay or not.

"All right, five more minutes, but then I will come and talk to you."

John looked peaceful. He was quite handsome; I always thought he looked like mum, but as we grew up without a father, I never knew what he looked like. Mum always told me I looked like her mum. Well, that was family that I never met.

I was just me, Hannah Reynolds, 27 years old, not very tall, just 1.63, with big blue eyes and blonde, shoulder-length hair. I was me, a child of God.

I went to his bed, put my head on his chest and cried like a baby. I told him how much I loved him and that I would be alright. I sat sobbing quietly, touching his face and holding his hand.

When Dr Parson came in, I looked up and begged him not to send me away, but with a soft voice, he told me it was time to leave.

For the last time, I hugged and kissed my brother.

Dr Parson told me to take a few days off. Even though I did not want to, I listened to him. This healing time, through crying and surrendering to the Lord, brought me to a new road. The Lord rose inside me, giving me a hope, a desire, a purpose. I grew so fond of my job that it ended up being my life. Everything I did was done at the hospital.

It was a challenge, though, to deal with the pain. I had to do it slowly, over a period of time. I cried and cried when I was by myself and kept giving it to the Lord. And one day it got better. I felt at peace, and I felt I was not alone; I never was because the Lord was always with me. My pain was just a scar and it did not hurt anymore.

The Lord was such a good, loving Father. I moved into the new house that John had purchased but never got the chance to move into. Now it was mine. A two-bedroomed house and I was on my own. It was a new beginning, and for some reason, I did not feel alone. I drew closer to the Lord in the middle of all of those challenges. I have learned to fully trust him. He was all I had. My life moved into a different dimension; I moved into my little house and just enjoyed my work.

Life moved on. The memories were no longer painful; they were just reminders to get up and get going again. The Lord was so good and carried me through it all. It changed not only my perspective but my character and personality too. I was a new Hannah, in a way, and kept changing as I grew closer to the Lord.

***

The week in hospital passed slowly and I was getting better. I was back on my feet and waiting for my left arm to heal.

Then it happened – the challenging and the impossible and the new beginning – which, at the time, I did not know but would soon enough find out.

One night, I heard a noise in the opposite room and someone was brought in. I needed rest, so despite the disturbance, I finally managed to fall asleep again.

The next morning, a nurse named Betty was on duty. I had worked with her many times. She was part of my team, so I knew her well. I had to handle around 12-15 nurses at a time, and one of my responsibilities was to run Unit C under the supervision of the doctors.

"Hannah, who would have thought you would be here, hey?"

"But not for long! I will be out soon. Who is on duty today?"

"Dr Parson. He's his normal, happy self, and he'll be here shortly to see you."

"That's good. I like seeing all the familiar faces. Makes me feel as if I am still working."

"Yes, girl, yes."

Betty was a friendly girl and laughed a lot. She was very short and had long, black hair put up in a bun.

The door of the opposite room opened and Hannah caught a glimpse inside. She stretched over curiously and asked, "Who is next to me? Why were they brought in last night?"

Betty opened the windows to let some fresh air into the room. She turned around and giggled.

"Yes, you have a new neighbour! A very handsome young man. Poor thing was brought in as an emergency after a car crash. We always get the car crashes, don't we? It was a miracle that he was still alive, and if you ask me, it will be a miracle if he makes it.

Hannah's heart was filled with compassion, and out of the blue, she felt hope rising.

"He will make it," she said.

Betty smiled.

"Yes, you are our little miracle angel. He might have a chance next door to you. You keep helping patients get better!"

"It's the Lord, Betty! I keep telling you that the Lord can do miracles and he does. He is the great Healer."

It was a beautiful March day. Spring was here, and it looked pretty nice outside. When Betty had left the room, I decided to stand up next to my bed. I felt a little pain in my left arm, but that did not scare me.

With a little effort, I managed to put my feet on the floor. I really wanted to see who was next door. I always loved being there for the patients. Maybe, for me, it was a bit more than just being a nurse. I loved helping people and making a difference, going the extra mile and bringing a little hope and happiness to some of the lost souls trapped in the hospital. I helped them get better and return to their lives.

Over the years, it was heartbreaking to see some of the people dying, but I've learned to cry and give it all to the Lord, to accept His will, even when I do not understand it. And to trust God. Yes, we are back to trust. It was something I've learned and am still learning every day. I've learned to be there for grieving families but also to rejoice over the healing and recovery of those who are given another chance in life.

One step and another step and another one, and slowly I was walking. The moment I reached the door, my left foot slipped and I fell. Without intending to, I screamed.

Dr Parson, the duty doctor, ran and opened the door and was next to me in no time.

"Hannah! Hannah, I thought it must be you, getting impatient to return to work. But now you are the patient, you need to learn to be patient. You will have to listen to me or I will confine you to your room," he said with a smile.

Dr Parson, a short man with black hair and black eyes, was a very good doctor. He and Dr Bernstein worked in Unit C, the emergency wing of Green Bell Hospital. Dr Parson had dedicated his life to medicine and saving lives.

"How am I doing, Dr Parson? Seems I am wrapped up for Christmas! What is going on?"

Dr Parson helped me to go back to bed and then sat next to me and took my hand in his.

"Hannah, you were in a car crash. It was not your fault, as you might know. But you will have to take it slowly. You know what I mean, healing and recovery. It will take as long as you want it to take, girl. You know that! Consider it a holiday for a few days."

I made a face.

"All right, I will listen to my doctor, but that does not make me happy. You know that."

Dr Parson gave me a hug.

"You will be fine! I will miss working with you, but you will be back in no time."

"Dr Parson, may I ask a favour?"

As he was about to leave, he looked at me, knowing what I was about to say.

"Yes, Hannah. When you are better, you can visit your neighbours. Just remember you are not a nurse for now."

"Thank you. Can I ask who is opposite me, in number 12?"

Dr Parson smiled sadly.

"A young man named Jack. He hardly made the night. But at least he is stable." Then he whispered, "He might need your prayers and angel touch."

After the doctor left, I prayed for the patient. His name was Jack. Interesting! I kept him in my prayers quite a lot, for some reason.

It was hard not to be working, but I had a few really good days. I managed to sleep and read, and Laura came to see me. Many other friends, mostly from the hospital, came to visit as well. However, something was missing; I felt something was slowly changing in my heart.

It always starts with the heart, it's true.

Back to Jack, I had a strong desire to meet the young man. I could not explain it, but I wanted to know how he was doing. My patience was pretty good, and I did not mind waiting. I knew the Lord had Jack in his hands and was looking after him. The Lord was good and merciful.

Chapter 2

Back to work

Hannah got through the next day with difficulty, wishing she could get back to work, but she decided to listen to the doctor. She knew resting would help her recover and she would be out in no time.

Laura Baker, her housemate and closest friend, came to see her. She was like family to her after sharing the house for almost five years. It had been too lonely for her to live alone after John's death.

At around 5 pm, she heard the emergency bell. Her normal reaction would have been to hurry and answer, but she remembered that she was not currently a nurse. God really had a sense of humour, slowing her down. I guess she did need a break,

---

Ephesians 6:18

Praying at all times in the Spirit, with all prayer and supplication. To that end keep alert with all perseverance, making supplication for all the saints.

otherwise she would have worked too much. At her age, who would not feel invincible?

She heard Dr Parson rushing along to Jack's room with a few nurses. She decided to pray and asked God to have mercy on Jack. When she had peace in her heart, she fell asleep thinking of him. She did not know much about Jack, but she was sure that once things improved and she was better, she would be learning a lot about him.

She woke up in the middle of the night and pressed the bell as she felt hungry. One of the nurses doing the night shift came in.

"Hello, Robbie."

"Hello, Hannah," said the young man.

"I am hungry, and I was wondering if I could have something to eat."

"At this hour? Yes, of course; let me look after you. I might find some biscuits or a yoghurt." He laughed.

It settled her down and she slept pretty well. In the morning, she asked Betty what day it was as she had lost track of the days. Betty was very kind as usual and spent a few minutes with her, telling her about the new patients and doing the usual things: blood pressure check, heart rate, temperature. Hannah felt like a baby.

Dr Parson came in a few minutes later and was happy to see that she was doing better.

"Robbie told me that you were a bit hungry in the night, which is good. Let's see how you are doing. Let me take a look at your arm."

One of the nurses removed the bandage and the doctor saw it was not red and swollen anymore; there was just a small bruise.

"I will apply only a little bandage today, what do you say, girl?"

"Thank you, doctor. May I ask about my neighbour, Jack?"

Dr Parson smiled and looked at me.

"Once you are back on your feet, you can look after him. He is stable, which is a miracle. Yesterday, we got five more in the unit and two went home. We are busy, so get well and get back, Hannah."

Hannah smiled sadly as she looked back into the past. She was a fighter, and she would fight for every life. The Lord was slowing her down to show her things, and she wanted to learn, to discover His will and plan. What was the new challenge, and how far would she be stretched this time?

On the other hand, her desire to find out about this young man, Jack, was growing slowly. What was his story, and how did he end up in Green Bell Hospital? There was a knock on the door.

"Excuse me!"

"Yes, come in," answered Dr Parson.

"Dr Parson, I am Matthew Miller, Jack's father. I was wondering if I could talk with you."

"No problem, Pastor Miller."

Jack's father was of medium height, with very gentle eyes and a soft voice. He was a kind and patient man, but his blue eyes betrayed sadness.

The doctor excused himself, but before he left, he touched Hanna's hand and whispered, "I'll see you later, girl!"

Hannah looked at Jack's father, thinking she had seen him somewhere before. He was a preacher, so maybe it was at some conference a few years ago.

Betty came in, and she took the opportunity to ask her.

"Was that Jack's father?"

"My, my! You miss your work, don't you? It would be good to have you back at work, and Jack needs your angel touch."

"Oh, I am sure you all did a great job, and the doctors are brilliant."

"Yes, his father is some sort of preacher, and you would probably like him. It's your thing. Jack's story is simple. I've heard that he and his friends were involved in a car crash when they were going home after a party. One of his friends was driving the car. All three ended up in hospital, but only Jack was brought to Unit C as he needed the best." She smiled proudly. Then she took a big, deep breath. "I feel

so sorry for him; he seems like a nice young man."
Betty was always a good source of information and
she loved talking.

Hannah had been in her job for more than 10
years; she had learned so many things and was still
learning. She worked with the best and loved being
with people and looking after them.

Dr Parson always said she had a real gift. It
was no surprise she was a senior nurse. She knew as
much as a doctor, but she never wanted to become a
doctor; she loved being a nurse too much. She would
sometimes even challenge the doctors, and that was
something Dr Bernstein loved. He was a tall black
man who attended a charismatic church.

During the day, Hannah listened to a few
sermons, had some quiet prayer time and listened to
the Lord. It was a quiet day, and she walked up and
down the hall. She was ready to go to work but knew
the doctors would not discharge her yet.

Molly, one of the nurses who worked with her,
was delighted to see her and told her by the next
week she would be back at work. Everyone told her
the same thing.

As she walked down the hall, she asked Molly
whether Jack was allowed visitors.

Molly smiled.

"Yes, you are one of us; go on. For sure, you will
be allowed."

"It will be only 10 minutes."

She opened the door confidently and saw a young man lying in bed. He was attached to various machines that beeped all the time. She knew them so well; they were part of her life.

It might have been challenging for some people to see that situation, but not for Hannah. It was a normal view and something she knew how to deal with. She walked toward his bed slowly, looking at his face full of bruises and his bandaged head. His right arm and shoulder were also bandaged.

In her work over the years, she had seen people looking worse and recovering, so it was not something that scared her. She had a heart of love and compassion like her heavenly Father.

She saw a handsome young man with beautiful blonde hair, and he seemed to be quite tall and athletic. He was asleep.

She approached the bed and gently touched his hand; she felt hope rising. Her Lord was a Healer. Her God was the true God and He would look after Jack.

"Hello, Jack. I am Hannah. From now on, I will be your angel," she whispered. "You will be fine. Don't worry; I serve a big, loving God. My Father is the Great Healer. He is an amazing Father, and He is looking after you." She smiled.

Dr Bernstein came in and was not surprised to see her in Jack's room. "Where else could you be, Hannah?"

"True, true, Dr Berstein. I believe by next week I will be back to work."

"I am sure you will be. You are quite a remarkable young lady. What do you think of our new friend?"

"No problem at all; he will be fine. He is a fighter!"

Dr Bernstein was in his 50s and had a large, lovely family. He was tall and slim and loved running. He and Hannah loved to chat about God if they were on lunch break at the same time. He was passionate about music and also believed in God the Healer. Hannah was an encouragement to him. He had worked with her for many years, and he was the one who had given her the nickname "Angel" as he believed she had a special touch from the Lord.

At first, it was too much for Hannah to be called an "angel" and she felt a bit weird, but as she came to understand how the Lord was working and imparting His grace through her, she let the Lord lead her and work miracles through her. It was not her doing the healing but the Lord. She was just a nurse, doing her job and giving courage and hope. Sadly, some people did not make it, but her kind words brought comfort to many families who were mourning.

She was on a journey where the Lord was using her; she was discovering how kind and merciful He was and how amazingly He was working in each one's life. The Lord helped her navigate through life's challenges. More than that, she learned to draw near to the Father, experience peace, love and joy and impart them to others. She was overflowing with grace from the Lord, and she was there, just there, for each person in a different way.

Today was the first time she had met Jack, and now that she could put a face to his name, she knew how to pray. She was there for him as Hannah as she was not back to work yet. For the majority of people, she would be Nurse Hannah, but also prayer angel Hannah who would go home and pray for each of her patients and colleagues, not only her friends. But for Jack, for now, she was just Hannah, his angel. Did he know that?

What really mattered was that she was there for him.

Over the next few days, she kept thinking of him and visited him daily, but he was never awake. She would stay a few minutes and speak to him in a whisper, and then she would leave. She knew that patients like him would sleep a lot as that was part of their healing. He was stable and had started to eat a bit, but the nurses said that he was very tired and did not stay awake for more than a few minutes.

Of all the patients, she was most interested in Jack. His journey of recovery would last for a few months, so she would have lots of time to look after him.

That was actually up to God. First, she would have to be back at work, and that would be only once she was fully recovered. She knew that not being fully recovered meant that complications might arise. Taking a day at a time was very important for Hannah.

Chapter 3

Don't give up!

Hannah was right; she was back at work in no time. Nothing could stop her, and the Lord answered her prayer to return to work.

It was a Monday morning and very cold as it had rained all weekend. It was wet and windy and was still dark outside. Hannah did the rounds with Dr Parson, then started her morning duties. She had 15 nurses under her command, and she knew what she was doing.

Hannah was very careful with each patient; she knew their files and worked well with the other nurses. Only her light blue uniform set her apart from the others. It matched her beautiful blue eyes and suited her blonde hair.

Philippians 2:4
Let each of you look not only to his own interests, but also to the interests of others.

One of the nurses told her to have a break as she had been very busy looking after patients. For Hannah, a little break of 10 minutes was usually spent in someone's room, checking the patient. Even her lunch break was snatched at moments when it was not busy. The nurses did not question her; they sometimes found her a bit weird, but amazing. She touched hearts in a different way, just by being there. She might have done things in a way that not many people understood, but we are all different in Christ; we each have our own identity and path in life. Hannah knew the best way to live her life and use all her gifts for God's glory, to impart grace and do good. She was a spark of light bringing hope into the world, so dark and lost.

For her 10-minute break, she entered Jack's room. He was asleep and nothing had changed during the past week. She had not yet seen him awake. Not even for 10 minutes.

She touched his hand and whispered, "Hello Jack. It's Hannah, How are you today?"

As she looked at him, she wondered what colour his eyes were and how his voice sounded. For a moment, her heart felt music. It was music she heard but did not understand. She felt a bit embarrassed and moved around the bed doing things.

"You know, it's very cold outside; it's good you are here with me, nice and warm and cosy."

Then she arranged his blanket, even though it did not need arranging, as the nurses were in and out all the time.

Jack heard her voice and recognized it. This time, he opened his eyes and saw her. It was Hannah, the pretty nurse who always talked to him about how much God loved him. He did not know what to say to her. As soon as she turned around and came toward him, he pretended he was asleep. He kind of liked her to pop in each day and looked forward to her visits. But what would you say to an angel like her?

Out of blue, she said to Jack, "Yesterday, I read a beautiful verse in John 19 and I was thinking of sharing it with you. You know, Jesus loves us and is so good to us. Jesus loves you. He is always here with you and He is your healer. We do not give up, do we?"

As she continued speaking, she did not hear someone knocking and opening the door. It was Matthew, Jack's father.

He was touched by Hannah's words and was filled with hope for his son. His eyes brimmed with tears as he looked at his son lying there. Only God could heal him. He decided to make a noise.

"Hmm... excuse me, I just knocked at the door and came in. Am I interrupting?"

"No, no, I just had a little chat with Jack. He is always asleep when I am around. Maybe he will be awake next time I come in."

She looked different from what he had expected. She had beautiful blonde hair put up in a little bun and a big, beautiful smile. She was not very tall, but her eyes were sparkling and filled with joy. This was Hannah!

"I am Hannah. You must be Jack's father."

"Nice to meet you, Hannah. I am Matthew. Yes, I am Jack's father."

Matthew did not know what to do, but Hannah knew that when visitors or family were around, it was time to go.

"I am doing my rounds, so I will leave you to spend some time with your son. Maybe he will wake up in a few minutes."

"Thank you, Hannah. You and the nurses are doing such a good job, and the doctors are very good. Thank you for looking after Jack."

Matthew took a chair and sat down next to his son's bed.

Jack was never awake when he visited, and he did not speak to him. He was not sure what he would say to his son. He just wanted him to get well and come home. There had been too many things between them over the past few years, and it was too much for him. This accident had come as a wake-up call for Matthew.

On the other hand, Jack was not ready to speak to his father. It was best to pretend he was asleep. He felt hurt and confused, and he needed time. And for sure, in hospital, he had time.

Hannah left the room and got busy. Later, while she was with another patient, the emergency bell rang and a panel on the wall outside showed it was coming from Jack's room.

Hannah and two other nurses headed that way.

His father, Matthew, was not in the room; he was talking with Dr Parson in the doctor's office.

Dr Parson rushed to Jack's room. Matthew heard Hannah saying something that touched his heart.

"Come on, Jack! Don't you dare to give up!"

One of the nurses showed Matthew a little waiting room nearby where he sat thinking of his beloved son. He felt so powerless; only God could really save him. He could only pray, and he did manage to pray a few words. Could anybody pray when in distress like this? What was going on? He thought his son was recovering!

Jack was awake and his entire body was shaking; he seemed to be in pain. One of the nurses said, "He's having a convulsion!"

Hannah went straight to him and he looked at her. For the first time, she saw his eyes. They were beautiful, ocean-blue eyes, and one could get lost in their beauty. That was what Hannah would have done if she'd had time.

She took his hand and held it firmly. Then he threw up all over everything, including Hannah's uniform. He was shaking, and his hands and arms were rigid.

"Jack, you need to calm down. Look at me!" she said firmly but kindly as she held him with both hands.

When he stopped being sick, he looked around and saw the mess over his bed and everywhere. She took his hand in hers and repeated, "Jack. Calm down. It is all right."

Dr Parson, who was doing checks trying to figure out the cause of the convulsion, said, "Oh, no. It's a reaction to the drug. I've already given him a calmant. It should work in a few minutes."

The emergency bell went crazy again. "Hannah, you are on your own. I'll leave you with Robbie. You two, come with me. I am off to the next one! It's Maria; she just got here this morning. You know what to do, girl!" He left the room, followed by the other nurses.

Jack looked at Hannah, and he had stopped shaking.

"Robbie, we need to clean up this mess," said Hannah. "I will be here with Jack for a while. You sort out some things. Thank you."

"Yes, I will be back in a few minutes. I'll bring some clean bed covers."

The room was quiet, and Hannah monitored Jack. She came back and sat next to him, making sure he was calm.

For the first time, he spoke to her.

"Thank you, Hannah!" He had a very kind voice.

Looking at the mess he'd caused, he felt embarrassed and lowered his eyes.

"Look at this! I am sorry."

Smiling, she took a pack of wipes and started to clean his hand.

"It is alright. You had a reaction to one of the medications. I've seen worse things."

As she gently cleaned his face, she asked him, "Would you like to clean yourself?"

Their eyes met, and she stopped for a moment. With a quick movement, he took her by the wrist. Looking deep into her eyes, he said, "Why would you look after me? I do not deserve to have anyone looking after me, being kind to me. Why?"

Hannah realised she was very close to him. She could hear their breathing and feel the tension in the air. "Jack, I am a nurse. This is my job!"

"Of course!" he said sarcastically.

"But also, the Lord told me to pray for you. So I am here!"

For a moment, she did not move, even though she felt it was unwise being so close to a man. He let go of her wrist, and tears ran down his cheeks.

"You do not know me. I have been such a bad person the past few years. I turned into something I was not. I was running away from pain. When my mother died, I got lost. It hurt so much. I abandoned my church, my friends, my dad, and I was angry with God. I am a bad person." He cried and put his head down.

She gently touched his hair.

"Jack, we all do bad things sometimes. I lost a loved one too; it is a painful journey that we all have to go through. Healing takes time. You are not a bad person."

He leaned his head on her shoulder and started crying like a baby. She put her hand on top of his and comforted him in silence. Jack took her hand and held it like a treasure.

At that moment, Robbie came in, but seeing Jack was feeling emotional, he just whispered, "Maybe I will come again in 10 minutes."

Hannah whispered, "Jack, the Lord loves you, and the Lord is a good, loving Father and healer. The Lord is looking after you. Everything will be alright."

After a few minutes, Jack looked at her.

"I am sorry. I guess I embarrassed myself."

"No, Jack. Don't be. You need time to cry and heal. You need to spend time alone with the Lord."

"Yes, you keep telling me the Lord loves me. I guess with my father being a preacher, I should know that."

"Yes, He does love you. But you are on your own journey with the Lord."

She stood up, ready to leave.

"Will you be alright? I have to do the rounds, and I left my team alone. I will send Robbie to look after you."

He took her gently by the wrist.

"Can you please come back?"

"Of course. I always come and check on you. It's my job."

He looked at her, hoping for a better answer.

"Hannah, I meant come after your shift is over. Please come and talk to me. I will not forget what you did for me. It means more than you know." He did not let go of her wrist for a moment.

Hannah looked a bit surprised, but she nodded.

"I will come and see you." Their eyes met and she felt a sparkle in her heart.

Dr Parson knocked at the door.

"Hannah, can you give me a hand? We've just got three new people and things are moving. I need you to come and do an assessment. First get cleaned up – you have five minutes. Let's roll it, girl!"

Robbie came back and Hannah left him with Jack as she went to change her uniform.

Hannah knew better than any of them what it meant to lose a loved one. She had lost John, and there was nothing she could do. When the Lord called him, the loss was hard to bear, but maybe that was what had triggered her to fight harder for all the people brought into the hospital. It also brought her into an intimacy with the Lord that not many experience. Through suffering we are made perfect! She had been through a lot but would not have changed anything as it brought her healing, love, joy and peace. She knew and felt the love of a Father who was caring for her through each one of the challenges.

Dr Parson looked at his senior nurse.

"You are an amazing nurse, Hannah. Well done!"

As they left the room, there was another emergency call.

"Go and talk to Matthew," Dr Parson said. "He has been waiting more than an hour. I can look after this one. I will beep if I need you. Just don't stay long." He smiled.

Hannah searched for Matthew and found him sitting sadly on a chair.

He stood up respectfully and saw Hannah smiling.

"Are you all right, Matthew?"

"Yes, I am all right. But how is Jack?"

"He is fine now."

"I thought I'd lost my son." He had tears in his eyes.

Hannah took his hand in hers and said boldly, "With God fighting for him, you will not lose him.

With God, all things are possible, hey, Pastor Miller?"
She sat on a chair next to him to keep him company.

"Hannah, I don't want to lose my son!"

"Matthew, God is good. Jack just had a reaction to one of the medications. He is fine. No matter what, I am not giving up on Jack. Are you?"

"Hannah, I need to get my son back. I lost him."

Before leaving, she whispered, "Fight for him in prayer and ask God to give him back to you. Just don't give up, Pastor Miller."

It was hard for Matthew. He had lost Jack, in a way, and the Lord was giving him one more chance.

He had almost given up on his son, but this unknown girl's passion for the Lord renewed his courage. Jack had not been himself for a few years, since Rosie, his mother, had died. Everything had crashed for Jack, and Matthew could not do anything. He tried to talk to Jack, he prayed, he did his best, but he felt it was not good enough. Matthew could only wait upon the Lord to bring his son back.

It had been a long wait, and he had almost lost hope.

Chapter 4

Friendship

Matthew left that day with new hope, faith rising in his heart and the chance of a better life not only for him but for Jack as well.

The sun was rising! It was a new day!

He met his best friend, Jacob Right. Jacob had worked at Northgate Church for many years and sometimes preached on Sundays. He was part of the leadership team and did a lot of volunteering as well. He was at the church most of the week.

"Hey, Matthew, how is Jack?" he asked his friend.

Matthew sat down at his little office table and was quiet for a few minutes. The office was a large room with a few tables which were shared by all the leaders and staff. Only Matthew had his own as he was there all day, coming and going.

---

2 Timothy 4:7
I have fought the good fight, I have finished the race, I have kept the faith.

Finally, he looked at his friend and answered, "Jack is doing better than me!"

"Is he? You spoke to him?"

"No, but he is doing much better, trust me."

Jacob was confused and waited to hear more.

"You know, I met that nurse today; I told you about Hannah. She really inspired faith and hope in me. The words she spoke made me think the Lord had sent her to wake me up, as if I was in a coma."

Knowing his friend was not a person to be moved easily, Jacob looked at his friend in surprise.

"Really, was she like an angel?"

"Actually, the staff and everyone call her "Angel". They gave her that nickname. She is a senior nurse and I've spoken with her before. Today, just before I left, there was an emergency when Jack had a reaction to one of the medications. The doctors and nurses looked after him and he is fine now, quite stable. But she came and spoke with me in the waiting room. She told me not to give up on my son. To fight in prayer!"

"She doesn't seem to give up!"

"No, she did not give up and she stood up as a fighter for my son. I almost gave up, but she did not. I believe she is an angel for me as well, in a way. It's amazing how gracious the Lord is and how he works. Praise the Lord."

After a few more hours at the church office, Matthew drove home. He stopped in front of his three-bedroomed house, opened the wooden gate and parked the car. It felt so lonely without Jack. He went straight upstairs and stopped in front of Jack's room. He slowly opened the door and went in.

He used to be tidier than he was now. During the past few years, he had lived in a total mess. It had all happened at once. He sat on Jack's bed and looked at a picture of Rosie. Jack looked a lot like his mother. He had the same lovely blue eyes and slightly messy blonde hair. He was a mini version of Rosie. He missed his son and he missed Rosie.

She had been a funny, kind and loving wife. They had been such a happy family till the news came that she had cancer and had only a few months to live. Everyone prayed, the church, family and friends. Jack prayed harder than anyone, but the Lord took her to heaven. It was heartbreaking for all of them, but for Jack, it was devastating.

Jack became quiet and gradually stopped communicating and going to church. He used to help in the church and had been involved with the worship. Then no more.

He still had his job in the bank but made some new friends who kept him out all weekend partying.

The only thing Matthew knew to do was pray. But was there any hope in his prayers? Any hope for his son?

There were ups and downs. Some days he felt it would get better, but he asked the Lord desperately for evidence, to open a new door, touch Jack's heart and bring him back.

He tried to talk to his son but obviously did not do a good job; he hardly spoke more than a few words a day to Jack. He counselled so many people, but he could not help his own son. He did not want to be helped.

A couple of weeks ago, when Jack and his so-called friends were coming back from yet another party, the car, driven by one of his friends, was involved in a crash. They were hit by another car and all of them ended up in hospital.

Matthew felt things were hopeless, but God, in his infinite mercy, had shown up amazingly and brought comfort and a new beginning in such an unexpected way.

Hannah kept her word and faithfully checked on Jack during her shift. She even made enquiries when she was not there. Usually, when her shift was over, she would stay a while just to spend some time with the nurses, helping and being there for the patients. Now, after visiting a few others, she would spend more time with Jack, talking to him and looking after him.

Dr Berstein, of course, knew about it and granted her permission to stay the extra minutes. Green Bell was a Christian hospital, after all. More than 20 years ago, a lady had left, in her will, all her fortune for the building of a big hospital with Christian values and a high standard of care. It had been built by Christian volunteers, and it was amazing how the Lord was working!

The nurses did not consider Hannah "obsessed with her work", as others who did not know her might have. But her colleagues learned a lot from a senior nurse like Hannah; it was not a job, it was her calling, her passion.

The doctors in the Emergency Department, Unit C, looked up to her as she came up with amazing ideas and ways of dealing with a situation. She received flowers and thank-you cards every day from patients who had been in the hospital. The Lord had blessed them and was working in their lives.

Some people did not understand her, but that did not bother Hannah. She was who she was, and she was not afraid of failure. She kept going, never looking back but moving forward with confidence, learning from mistakes and striving for the impossible. She certainly loved challenges.

She knew that prayer was the key to open doors. Waiting for God's answer and accepting God's will were important as well. She would fight for each patient, but if the Lord took them, she would submit to His will.

Some of the nurses liked to pray as she did, but others did not. Hannah understood and respected their choice of wanting or not desiring a relationship with the Lord. Not everyone was chosen.

"Hello, Jack. It's me, Hannah, again." He opened his eyes.

"Hello, Hannah. So glad to see you."

She smiled and tried to avoid his eyes.

"How was your day?"

"Come on, Jack, you do not want me to tell you about the hospital and my work. It might be boring." With one move, she let her hair down and shook it onto her shoulders.

Jack looked amazed and laughed.

"You are beautiful, you know that?"

"Come on, Jack, you always tease me!"

He was very serious, and their eyes met.

"Hannah Reynolds, you are beautiful!"

She smiled, got a chair and sat next to him.

"Thank you!"

He was doing much better and no longer had bandages around his leg; only his shoulder and arm were still wrapped up. His beautiful fair hair suited his ocean-blue eyes that, in the past few weeks, had got their sparkle back.

Hannah read him a beautiful story about Elijah, and he said, "Now let's hear what you think about it. You always have amazing thoughts."

"You know, I was thinking, if you read carefully, Elijah and Moses were on similar journeys. Moses spent 40 years in the desert where the Lord prepared his heart, and then he was called to go back on the same road. He was strong, and God was with him. Elijah was the same; he went back on the same road. In a way, we all go back to go forward. We all go on the same road. What about you, Jack? Which road are you on?"

"I am starting to figure it out. Not sure yet; not sure, Hannah."

She put her hand gently on his and then opened the Bible at Psalms.   "I always love the psalms. My cat Benny loves them too." Looking again at Jack, she carried on. "Did I tell you today how much God loves you, and your friends too, and that your father misses you?"

"Yes, Hannah, you always tell me that." He smiled and touched her hand.

"What about your father? Did you speak to him?"

Jack grew quiet and stood up slowly from the bed. He walked toward the window.

"No, Hannah, I did not!"

"Why, Jack?"

He was looking out the window and did not want to speak to her; it was very quiet in the room for a few minutes.

"He is your father and he loves you." Realising there was no point in staying, she said softly, "I think I'd better leave, Jack."

He still did not move or say anything. She took her jacket and bag and walked toward the door. Looking at him sadly once more, she just added, "Goodbye."

Once the door had closed, he turned his head and said aloud, Jack, Jack. You know she is right. Why are you fighting with everyone?" He took a deep breath, which was painful.

Dr Bernstein saw Hannah leaving and approached her for a chat.

"Dr Bernstein, I am tired. I believe I will go home. I have a late shift tomorrow."

"Get some rest, girl. You should be at home already. I am in tomorrow, so see you then!"

That night, Jack could not sleep. He kept thinking of Hannah and also his father. She was right; his father was a very good father, but he had blown it during the past years and stopped talking to him. It was painful for him, but he had to deal with certain things. He spent time in prayer and cried bitterly as he went back into the past, asking God to heal him and help him move on. It was not the time to wrestle with the Lord but to let the Lord work in his life and to follow the path laid in front of him.

As soon as the morning came, he called the doctor.

"Dr Bernstein, I know you will be leaving soon. Would you please call my father? I would like to see him."

The doctor looked surprised.

"But you saw him yesterday, did you not?"

Jack said sadly, "There are some things I need to sort out. It's very important for me to see him today."

"All right, son, all right. I will call him."

Dr Bernstein called Pastor Miller, who was very surprised to get a phone call so early in the morning.

"Hello, Pastor Miller. This is Dr Bernstein, from the Green Bell Hospital. It's nothing for you to worry about."

"Hello, Dr Bernstein."

"Jack is fine. I just had a chat with him and he asked me to give you a call. He wants to speak with you. He said it was important."

After a moment of quietness, he said, almost whispering, "He wants to see me?"

"Yes, Matthew. I am just finishing my night shift, so I'm giving you a call now as I am about to go home."

"Thank you, I understand."

Matthew was filled with joy and overwhelmed by the Lord's grace and favour, by his goodness and love, and shared this with his friend Jacob.

"The Lord is so good to me, Jacob. He granted me and my son another chance, not only with each other as a family but for Jack to have a better life. It has been so hard for him after we lost Rosie."

"That is very good news, Matthew."

"And he wants to see me, which is good."

He went to the hospital and opened Jack's door. Jack tried to smile; he knew he was not looking quite so lost.

His eyes still looked tired, but he seemed more himself.

"Hello, Dad. I am really glad you came."

Matthew leaned over, gave him a hug and took a chair near his bed.

"How are you, Jack?"

"I am better. I am still here."

"That is great, son. Very good!"

Matthew was so happy to see his son but was not sure what to say. He knew his visiting time was limited and his son needed to rest and recover.

"Dr Bernstein called me this morning really early, saying that you wanted to see me."

"Yes, Dad."

"Jack, you know I am here for you."

Jack put his head down and gathered his all energy to speak.

"Dad, I had to see you. I had to say I am sorry. I've been a jerk since Mum died. It was too much for me and I felt deserted by God and everyone. It felt so unfair to lose Mum. I loved her so much and it hurt so much to lose her. Can you forgive me?"

Matthew did not say anything; he just listened to his son, who had tears in his eyes.

"I would like to try again – me and you. Could you give me another chance?"

Matthew also had tears in his eyes, and he gave him another hug.

"Jack, you are my son and will always be my son, good or bad. I am sorry too! I guess I did not do a good job the past few years after Mum went to be with the Lord. Of course we can try again, hey, Jack?"

They both smiled and had a sense of peace. Matthew hugged his son and held him for a moment.

There was a knock at the door, and Hannah entered.

"I can come in five minutes, all right?" she said, realising she had interrupted an emotional moment.

Jack spoke slowly.

"Hannah, please do not go!"

"All right, Jack, but I need to do my usual checks for you."

Matthew said, "You and the nurses are doing such a good job. Soon Jack will be going home!"

"Thank you. We are doing our best."

Suddenly the emergency bell rang and Hannah said, "I'll be back later. Enjoy the time with your dad." She rushed out the door and did not come for the rest of the day. The other nurses came and went, but Jack felt something was missing. He wondered whether she would come back or not.

At 7 pm, the end of Hannah's shift, he heard a knock at the door and Hannah came in.

She looked tired and she did not want to stay long, but she did want to see Jack.

"Hi, Jack."

"Hannah, I'm so happy you came."

She took a chair nearby and slumped onto it.

"I am going home soon. I just came to check on you to make sure you are ok. The nurses and the doctors did a good job."

"Yes, thank you. And I had a good day with my dad. You look so tired."

"Good! I'm so glad you met your father."

"Hannah!" he said as she was not looking at him.

"Hannah!" As he said her name the second time, she looked him straight in the eye.

"Yes, Jack!" She smiled at him.

"I was rude to you yesterday. And you left."

"It's ok. Nothing wrong happened. You needed some time for yourself. I understand."

"I am sorry. I should not have let you go away. You are always so good to me."

They looked at each other for a while, neither saying anything.

Then Hannah said, "I forgive you! I cannot be upset with you, can I?"

"That is sweet of you, Hannah!" He looked at her with admiration.

"Jack, I won't be able to see you tomorrow. Betty will look after you, as well as Robbie and a few other nurses. He looked puzzled and shook his head.

"I am working in Unit B. They need a senior nurse, and there you go. I won't be able to come and see you."

"When will I see you again?"

"I do not know. Maybe sometime this week. I am working in Unit B for a few days."

"I need to see you. Please come again!"

She stood up to leave and could not look at him. She felt a bit emotional. She would cry if she stayed longer. He gently touched her hand.

"Please come!"

She did not look back and left without saying a word. It was dark and she was looking forward to a shower and her bed.

***

I was so happy that Jack had survived and was so thankful to the Lord for giving this young man another chance. He and his dad seemed to have had a good chat. It made me feel as though I was being used by the Lord to impart grace and love and joy.

The next day I would be working in another unit and would not see him. Of all the patients, I would miss him the most. I looked after him even after hours and it would be good to see him.

Actually, let's be honest. I wanted to see him. During the past weeks, after my shift, I had spent not just 10 minutes with him but more like an hour or so. I had got to know a bit about Jack Miller and, for sure, I enjoyed his company. Maybe a bit too much.

Well, I was too tired to think anymore, but I shared my good news with Laura, who was so happy when I told her that I had a patient who had become a bit special to me. Laura did know about Jack, and she smiled and looked at me, puzzled.

"Special? Let's be serious. You like being with him and spending time with him. You are, in a way, like good friends."

"True. But I am afraid I might enjoy his company too much!"

"Why? What would be wrong with having someone in your life?"

"Fall in love? *Me?* You must be joking!"

"Yes, have a private life of your own and don't work so much."

"Well, maybe I am not ready for love and a relationship. And I certainly haven't thought about or prayed for those things lately."

"Jack is a very good friend and you enjoy his company. And he enjoys yours, you tell me. Let's see what the Lord will bring next for you two. Friendship or friendship becoming a deep love?" She laughed and Hannah looked at her with big eyes. It was something that she didn't think about. But she had thought of Jack a lot lately.

Chapter 5

What is next?

Hannah was busy the rest of the week and did not have time to visit Jack at all. She had been working extra shifts as Unit B required extra staff. She had worked in other units before, mostly Unit B, and the staff and doctors there had a lot of respect for her. Being a senior nurse, she was pretty good at dealing with the stress; it did not bother Hannah if there were extra patients and bells ringing. She knew how to do her job calmly, with precision, and she was a good leader, but she also worked hand in hand with the nurses. No matter the work required, she was there.

The truth is she wanted to have a break from meeting Jack as she felt he was getting too close to

---

John 14:27

Peace I leave with you; my peace I give to you. Not as the world gives do I give to you. Let not your hearts be troubled, neither let them be afraid.

her heart. Actually, he was in her heart in a way, and that was something she did not want to deal with.

However, Jack was improving and he was determined to be fully back on his feet soon. He listened to the advice of Dr Bernstein and Dr Parson, who had more than 30 years of experience in recovery procedures.

His old friend Mike visited him a few times. He was his friend from high school, but when Jack had gone astray a few years ago, they had stopped meeting. Having found out from Matthew that Jack had asked about him, he visited him in hospital and they got back on track with their friendship. Mike was a very nice young man who worked for a company dealing with planning and road works. He was engaged and had been attending Northgate Church for years.

Matthew decided to give Hannah a call and phoned the hospital, Unit B, where she was working.

"Hello, Hannah. This is Matthew. How are you?"

"I am fine, thank you. I have been a bit busy working. I am in Unit B at the moment. How are you?"

"I am fine, thank you. I was wondering when I would see you back on Unit C."

"It might be another week, I'm not sure, but I will try to pop around one of these days. I've heard you and Jack are back on track. You must be very proud of your son!"

"Yes, he is recovering very well. He might be home soon."

"I will try my best to come and visit soon. All my best to Jack."

The days passed very quickly and Jack wondered when Hannah would come. He just kept going and doing his best. He started praying again, drawing near to the Lord and moving in the right direction. He seemed to rise up like an eagle and get stronger each day. His father was very proud of him, and a few of the church members came to say hi. Deep down in his heart, he kind of missed her. She had presented him with quite a challenge while he had been in hospital. The Lord seemed to have brought Hannah into his life with a purpose, and it was not always easy.

Things were getting better, and he felt more and more confident that he was on the right track. Healing and restoration were taking place in his heart, his life and his relationships.

Hannah and her words restored faith in his heart and raised his hopes, and the Lord opened his eyes. His life was going in the right direction, but a different one. He started to change. Yes, he changed.

He kept wondering whether she was still upset with him or why she would not visit him. He missed their conversations and the way she made him laugh. He could not remember the last time he had laughed, but she always made him laugh. She was so intelligent, too, and he loved talking with her. She was beautiful and so was the smell of her hair. She was in his heart.

On Friday at around 3 pm, he heard a knock on his door. He was sitting in his chair reading, dressed in a t-shirt and a pair of jogging bottoms.

Thinking it was one of the nurses, he answered, "Come in!" but did not look up from his book.

"Hello, Jack!" came a familiar voice.

He almost jumped out of his chair. His heart filled with emotions and his eyes sparkled.

"Hannah!"

The young woman in front of him was not looking at all like a nurse. Her blonde hair was down on her shoulders and she was wearing a red t-shirt and a pair of jeans. She had a beautiful smile, and her warm blue eyes were filled with joy.

She put her bag on a chair and said again, "Hello, Jack!"

"Hello, Hannah." He smiled, still looking at her in amazement.

"You look… You look beautiful!"

"Thank you. So, I do not look like a nurse anymore?"

"It's so lovely you came," he said.

He stood up and walked around. He was still a bit hesitant with his left leg but was fairly confident.

He was walking like a man who wanted to show he was on the road to recovery.

"You are doing very well, the doctors and nurses told me. A few more days and you'll be going home."

He offered her a chair and showed her the book he was reading. His hand touched hers and she looked at him for a moment, then shyly lowered her eyes. He smiled, with his heart overflowing. They started chatting like good friends. They both loved reading, and they laughed as they ended up quoting the same favourite Bible verses.

Pastor Matthew also came to visit Jack, but when he heard that Hannah was there, he decided to go down for a coffee in the hospital restaurant.

Back in Jack's hospital room, the two young people were having so much fun. They suddenly stopped laughing and looked at each other. Hannah became embarrassed and turned her eyes toward the window.

Out of blue, he said, "When are you back on Unit C?"

"I'm sorry, but I have been very busy and I'm working extra shifts. Today is my day off, so, as I promised, I came to see you."

Jack looked at her and without hesitation said, "I have been waiting for you. Hannah, I have been praying for you!"

"Thank you, Jack. I have been praying for you, too. However, this is my job and I have to work."

He realised he had gone a bit too far and backed off a bit.

"Yes, of course, you have lots of patients to look after. Maybe when I am out of the hospital, I'll be able to see you? May I?"

"Yes, I guess so." She did not know what to say.

At that moment, the door opened and Matthew entered the room.

"Hello, Hannah! You look quite remarkable, young lady! I hardly recognized you."

"Doesn't she look beautiful?" Jack smiled, looking at his dad.

Hannah laughed. "You've already told me that three times, thank you, Jack."

Turning to Matthew, she said, "You have a brave son here. He will be out in a few days."

Jack walked across the room and looked out of the window. He would be lost in the world outside. He felt sad and did not want to leave.

He realised he wouldn't be able to see Hannah and he was going back to an empty house. Well, it would be he and his father, but they had lots of issues to deal with. He wanted to go home, but he would miss Hannah. And yes, he was looking forward to going back to work. What about Hannah? When would he see her? Did she really want to meet him again? Maybe he was just another patient. Maybe not.

Lots of thoughts came and went as he looked out the window, lost and unsure of tomorrow.

His father noticed and said, "Maybe you could come and visit our church, Northgate Church. What do you say?"

"I would love that!"

"Maybe you could come for dinner – what do you think?" Jack asked very directly, turning around and walking slowly toward Hannah.

"Thank you; that will be nice. However, I do work a lot!" She hesitated, very surprised by Jack's invitation.

"Please say yes!" He looked at her and their eyes met.

He took her hand in his and held it tightly but gently as though he did not want to let her go

She felt shy and put her head down.

"I've already said I would come for dinner."

As she left, Pastor Miller took a visiting card from his pocket and gave it to her.

"I am sure you know where the church is, but anyway, you can have my phone number as well. But I guess you have them at the hospital. Well, this is a bit different. You are not invited as a nurse."

Hannah looked at Jack and did not know how to say goodbye. She stretched out her hand politely.

Jack came closer and said gently, "Would you mind if I gave you a hug?"

"No…!"

He put his big arms around her and hugged her, and for a moment, he could hear music. It was music to his heart. Music in his heart. Yes, it was love. She felt the same, and she wished time would stand still. It was something she'd never felt before and she was not sure how she would handle it. It felt as if they were hugging for a long time, but it was only a few seconds.

Matthew felt a bit out of place and smiled.

She left and the two of them were alone in the room.

"Dad, I believe that I like Hannah – a bit too much!"

"Son, I believe that she is an admirable young lady. Jack, you need to take it more slowly; otherwise, you might end up with a broken heart."

Jack looked at his dad and smiled.

"Yes, and no. But you're probably right. I've never met anyone like her. She is totally adorable and amazing. She is Hannah!"

"You are in love, Jack!"

He smiled.

"Yes, I am, Dad. I am in love."

The day soon came when the doctors told Jack that he could return home.

He was happy but sad. He had not seen Hannah for almost a week; she had popped in just a few times for a short chat after she had finished work in the other unit. He wanted her to stay longer and talk more with him. Maybe he scared her away; maybe it was too much for her; maybe she was not interested in a guy like him.

Was he really special? The Lord God calls each one of us special, children of God. For him, it was not only walking again but starting his life again, and he wanted to move on. He was moving a bit too quickly, as his father had said. But it was like rediscovering himself. Part of him was being awoken, and he had new things to experience. He was ready and excited to go with the Spirit, to flow and walk in grace. But yes, patience and following the Lord were not always easy.

Since Jack had started to pray for her, a desire had started to form in his heart. A desire to see her, to be with her, to talk to her. Love, again love, growing like a flower in his heart and slowly blooming.

They were good friends and had lots of things in common but differed in others. But each moment was a treasure to him.

His father was probably right; he need not rush as he could end up with a broken heart if Hannah did not have the same feelings for him.

On the last day, Dr Parson kept giving him information. It was good that his father was listening because he was not. Where was Hannah? Why did she not come to see him? Had she forgotten him? Maybe he was not special to her; maybe he was just another patient. All kinds of thoughts and worries came and went and he wanted to leave as soon as possible.

The fear that is mentioned so often by people, the fear that is mentioned in the Bible, is not good. Is there fear in love? In the perfect love of God, there is no fear at all!

The love between a man and a woman is special and beautiful and the Lord blesses those who follow him wholeheartedly.

The doctor left, and he decided to talk to his father but did not know what to say or how to start.

"Dad, do you think Hannah will come?"

"Of course, son. Wait and see."

***

Dr Parson came again to say a short goodbye and remind me I would still have to come for regular checkups at the hospital. As I left the unit, I felt so sad. She had not come after all. She'd forgotten about me. Then I heard someone running behind me.

"Hey, Jack!"

"Hannah!"

I turned around and looked at her and my heart was filled with hope. Hannah, my Hannah, had come for me. She was there. My heart was so filled with love and joy that I just wanted to take her in my arms and walk away with her, but I did not.

"I thought you'd forgotten about me!"

"How can you say that? It does not mean, if I did not come to see you, that I did not pray for you or think of you."

I looked at her in surprise and was not sure whether to believe her or not.

"Really, you did?"

"Go home, Jack. Start your new life and be blessed. I am happy for you, Jack, and you too, Matthew. I wish you both all the blessings."

"Thank you, Hannah, for all you did for me and my son."

My dad gave her a short hug and smiled.

Not knowing what to do, I kept looking at her until she said, "Are you going to hug me or not?"

Without hesitation, I took her in my arms and held her tight. I did have feelings for her and could not hide them, at least not from myself. I had fallen in love with her. I could not hide it from her, either. It was not something that I'd planned. It was something I'd never considered. Love was the last thing that would have crossed my mind a few weeks ago.

The smell of her hair, her beautiful blue eyes and her gentle voice were all very appealing. She was a strong character and very direct. Funny sometimes, and challenging, with a bold, quick walk and a delicate feminine figure. Hannah, this was my Hannah. But was she mine? Was her heart mine? Probably not yet.

"Thank you, Hannah, for everything," I whispered. "God has brought me back to the right path. And you are *my* angel. You hear? *My* angel."

Tears welled in her eyes, and he noticed but did not say anything. She reacted a bit clumsily. "I will miss you, Jack!" Their eyes met, and she turned around, moved out of his arms and left. "Good bye."

I wanted to go after her, but Dad said, "Let her go, son. Give her some time. We need to go home, anyway. We'll talk later."

I was quiet in the car, even though my dad was very chatty and tried to talk to me. I was touched by Hannah's reaction and really wished I had gone after her. However, my dad might have been right. I needed to give her some time to figure out her heart and whether she really had the same feelings for me as I had for her.

A couple of days passed during which I mostly hung around at home, trying to reorganize my room, my thoughts, my life. I was taking it easy, slowly getting back on track and finding a *new* me.

I started jogging again and getting in touch with my old friends. I had moved on from the "party friends".

The best thing that happened was returning to church; it was great as so many people were so happy to see me. Well, I had grown up in church, in a way, so they all knew me.

One day, Mike popped around and we had a long chat. It was so good to have a friend who understood me. I was managing to do things in the house and even started to cook dinner. It was boring being at home, and I started hanging around at the church. I was stubborn, but at least I was out of the house.

***

One evening, Matthew started a conversation about love at the dinner table and Jack had no option but to join in.

"How are you, Jack? You are doing lots of things and have a new life and I am proud of you. However, you have been quiet lately regarding certain things?"

"Yes, Dad. True, Dad." I looked at my father. He was a very good dad, and he was such a gentle, kind man, a very good leader and very gifted. He was very patient, especially with me, and I needed that now. I was not patient with myself, though. It was quite hard, but I was enthusiastic about starting afresh.

"Are you alright, son?"

"Yes, Dad. I am kind of starting my life from zero. That is how I feel. I had a chat with Mike. I have been a bit quiet, and I am sorry. I don't want you to think I am ungrateful or rude."

"No, no, I just wanted to know if I could help you with anything or if you wanted me to pray for anything more than I am. I did not mean you are not talking to me; I just sense you have some things on your heart and want you to know I am here."

"Yes, many things. I am thinking of starting a project at church and want to do so many things: maybe play guitar in the worship band and possibly cut down my work at the bank to four days!"

Matthew looked at his son in surprise.

"You have been thinking a lot, son. That is good, but the doctor said to take it easy."

"I am, I am, but I want to move on with my life. I feel the Lord gave me a new chance, a new life, and I am really thankful and looking forward to living for his glory and imparting grace."

"Praise the Lord you are moving on! Are you sure you are, Jack?" he teased his son.

Jack got the joke and laughed too.

"Was I really so bad, Dad?"

He was serious but teasing a little as well.

"Yes, you were, at times!"

Jack laughed and they had a good time.

"Will you pray for me, Dad? I might need a special prayer, if there is such a thing."

"Of course, Jack. God hears all prayers, son. You are my son and I am here for you. And that is all you need help with? Nothing else for now?"

His father knew there was something else but was waiting for Jack to bring it up. He wanted to make sure he raised the subject when he was ready for it; otherwise, there was no point. Some people do not get it, no matter how many times you explain it to them, as they do not want to face the truth. The Lord does say, "I am the way, the truth and the life." The truth does set you free. And only the Lord can open the eyes of the blind.

"Dad, I've been thinking a lot about Hannah!"

"Yes, of course you have, son." His father smiled.

Jack felt embarrassed and smiled, hitting his dad gently on the shoulder. Then he found his courage and continued.

"I know what you are thinking! I have been thinking of her a lot. I miss her. I am in love with her. And who would not be? She is adorable, amazing."

"Yes, you are in love with her. Love is a beautiful thing! Love is amazing, if the person you are in love with shares the same feelings as you. You can share them together."

Jack looked at his dad.

"I would like to ask her for a date, but she might not look at a guy like me, and she is working all the time. I am getting out of a messy life and just getting back on the road after an accident. Not the best, am I?"

"Son, love does not speak of reason. Follow your heart. And if you really want to ask Hannah for a date, I would suggest praying and seeing what the Lord says; then follow your heart!"

"Alright, Dad. Alright."

"Jack, you are a handsome, intelligent young man, blessed and with a beautiful heart. Any girl would want to find such a treasure as you."

Jack looked at his dad, unbelieving.

"You say that because I am your son."

"Both, but I also know that in true love there is no fear. Pray and wait upon the Lord. I will back you in prayer. I already have."

"Thank you, Dad!"

Chapter 6

Northgate Church

Jack had been home for two weeks and time was flying for him. His life had begun anew. He returned to work at the bank and was offered a position as manager of one of the branches. This opportunity came as a blessing out of the blue.

But the Lord works in mysterious ways. He was not sure he understood it all the time but he had a new love for the Lord and a growing passion to follow Him.

He also started working on a family support project which he organised and developed with his friend, Mike Turner. Claire Black, who was also dedicated to serving, helped as well. Mike was engaged to Polly. He was a very patient young man, a good listener and a good friend.

Proverbs 16:3
Commit your work to the Lord, and your plans will be established.

Regarding Hannah, Jack was still praying and praying. The Lord was opening doors and changing things and redirecting him in all directions except Hannah. He did not know what to do or how to do it, so he was just waiting and, yes, missing her.

Maybe it was the end and the Lord had answered with His silence: it was a no. He had hardly any hope anymore. He was thinking that she had forgotten about him as she was busy working. She was surrounded by a lot of people, and for sure, many young men had a crush on her; she could do better than choosing him.

Even though his dad told him to be patient and wait for her, that she would contact him or come to church, he thought it might be best to stop praying for her the way he was and somehow move on. But deep down in his heart, he did not give up, despite so many worries and concerns. He wanted to see her and wanted to meet her and wanted to make a way in the impossible situation, so he kept praying.

It was a beautiful Sunday and Hannah was happy as she had been praying and was looking forward to visiting Jack and the church. She was, in a way, waiting as she had not yet decided and wanted to be sure the Lord did want her to go to Northgate Church.

She had said yes, that she would visit the church, so sooner or later she would have to keep her word.

Maybe it was more than a visit. Maybe it was something the Lord put on her heart. Laura kept telling her to go, but she kept finding excuses, and working was one of them. Then she used to go to her little church, which became, for Hannah, like a hiding place, small and secure. Northgate Church was different; there were not 50 people but 1000 or more. She was not even sure how she would handle something so out of her comfort zone.

***

Today was the day, and I was nervous. I was not sure what to wear, which was not quite me. I asked Laura, and she laughed and told me that I was anxious.

"Maybe I should not go. Rather go to my little church."

"No, no, you promised Pastor Miller and Jack."

"Yes, I did!"

"And I am sure Jack is missing you."

"Probably not. He is the son of the preacher, and I am just a little nurse, living my busy life. Did I tell you he works in a bank?"

"You see, you are thinking of him too!" She was right. I was praying and thinking of him and I missed our conversations.

Laura Baker, my lovely faithful friend for so many years, was already in a relationship and kept telling me to find myself someone, but I did not. She was totally opposite from me, in personality and looks, with brown eyes and chestnut hair. She was a pharmacist and worked at the same hospital. We often prayed together, although she went to another church. God brought us together, and we treasured our friendship.

"I cannot go!" I looked in the mirror.

"You look lovely in this beautiful blue shirt and your blue jeans."

I left feeling a bit unsure and somewhat pushed by my friend. I did want to go, but I was not sure what to expect. I had not spoken to Jack for a couple of weeks, and I did not know what to say to him, although I had so many questions. Praying about it was difficult, but I had prayed a lot for him. My heart was racing and my mind was flying. I managed to be on time at church, and I followed the people inside.

It was a beautiful church with a semicircular design at the entrance and front of the building. On the right were groups of kids and prayer groups and on the left some offices upstairs and the tea room downstairs. I said hello to a few people and found a place toward the back of the auditorium. I got a bit lost in the huge crowd, which was quite comforting.

The service started and I noticed that Jack was part of the worship team, playing a guitar somewhere at the back. I felt anxious, and I seemed to hear other music. It was music in my heart. I was at the right place. Yes, he had mentioned he played the guitar, but I had never heard him play.

Then Pastor Miller gave the sermon, a very good message from John 10 on the good shepherd and Jesus's love. The Lord is a good shepherd and directs our footsteps. I did feel directed there that day, and the sermon was definitely for me. I needed to be reassured by the Lord that I was in his will. I asked the Lord hundreds of times whether I should go to Northgate Church, and the answer was yes in so many ways. The service ended with a few announcements and prayers. A man who introduced himself as Joseph Morris announced a new project called Give Hope and called Jack Miller and Mike Turner onto the stage.

My heart started to beat rapidly, and I tried to sink into the chair as I was afraid, for some reason, he would see me. Why was I doing that? I had gone there to meet him, hadn't I?

Well, first I came to worship with his church and then to meet him. But this was not Green Bell Hospital, and I was out of my comfort zone. It was quite brave of me to go somewhere new. I had not seen or spoken to Jack before the service, and I was not a nurse, or his nurse, that day. I had become his friend. Yes, I felt I was his friend.

"Jack Miller and Mike Turner put together this project. They want to invite you to an afternoon of worship and prayer to launch the project, which you already know about. It will be presented in more detail, and you can get involved if you want to. As you know, the "prodigal son" has returned," Joseph laughed, "and the Lord is doing miracles through him. Thank you, Jack and Mike. Is there anything you'd like to add?"

Looking at him on the stage, I saw a handsome man, tall with beautiful blonde hair, dressed in a smart blue shirt, who had a very good voice. Was it the same man I'd looked after in hospital? He did not look frail but confident, bold. He was living his life.

"Thank you, Pastor Morris. Yes, I wanted to say a big thank you to the church and to Mike Turner, my dear friend, and my father, Matthew Miller, as well as Claire Black, who all worked so hard to put this project together. Next Saturday we will have a get-together – you are all welcome – and we will launch it. Thank you for your support and prayers, and we will see what doors the Lord will open and how far the Lord takes us. With the Lord all things are possible."

Then it was prayer time, after which everyone started leaving. I wanted to talk to Jack, but as I walked down one of the aisles toward the front of the church, I saw Jack surrounded by people, so it did not take much to change my mind. I turned around and left without looking back.

It had been a blessed Sunday and I was there; I had been afraid to talk to Jack, but at least I saw him.

As I left the building, I gave one of my visiting cards to one of the people greeting at the door. I wrote on the back, "Well done, Jack, on your project! God bless. Hannah."

***

Jack was still talking in the main auditorium with lots of people when one of the greeters came and gave him the card.

"Excuse me, Jack. A young lady left this card for you."

He took the card, and when he saw the name and the message on the back, he quickly excused himself and hurried out the door. He looked around the car park. It was huge, and he was not sure where to find her, with people leaving and cars driving out.

He was discouraged but closed his eyes and felt a sense of peace. He heard the Lord speaking to him, and when he opened his eyes, he spotted her. She was more than 10 metres away, but he called her name and started to run.

She turned her head as he caught up with her.

"Hannah, you came!"

"Hello, Jack!"

He gave her a big, tight hug, which he thought might have embarrassed her.

"I am so happy you came. I have been waiting for you."

"Have you?"

"Let me go and tell my dad. He will be so happy. Are you staying for lunch, or dinner?"

"Jack, I am working tomorrow. Maybe another time."

"Please stay. Please come for lunch. You cannot leave now; you've just come."

For a moment, she turned her head, and he was sure she would say no. His heart sank.

"All right, Jack, I will stay for lunch!"

"Sure? Is it yes?"

"Yes, yes, Jack, I will come for lunch."

"Let's go and speak with Dad and see what his plans are, and then I will show you where we live. What do you say?"

"That will be fine with me, Jack."

He took her hand but she withdrew it gently. Maybe he'd got a bit carried away. He felt as if he could fly, and for sure, his heart was flying. He was ecstatic that Hannah had come to see them, well, to see him. At that moment, he was sure that the Lord was saying 100% yes. It was a strong confirmation, and that was all he needed.

His prayers had been answered and the desires of his heart granted. The Lord had brought Hannah. Now it was about taking it a step at a time. That was the hard part for Jack as he was not very patient and he was in love.

Chapter 7

The Millers' house

As Jack entered the church with Hannah, his dad was ready to leave and walked toward them.

"I've found her, Dad!"

"Oh, Jack, you might scare away our lovely Hannah!" His dad smiled, teasing his son.

Looking at her, he added, "Hello Hannah. It was nice that you joined us today at church."

"Thank you, Pastor Miller. It was a lovely service!"

As Claire Black and Joseph Morris were leaving, they stopped next to Jack.

"So, this is Hannah, your angel?"

Hannah smiled and said hello.

"Yes, she is my angel." He introduced Hannah to both of them.

Proverbs 14:1
The wisest of women builds her house, but folly with her own hands tears it down.

Claire was in her late 60s and was part of the church staff.

"We've heard quite a lot about you, that you looked after our Jack in hospital."

"Yes, I am a nurse, but God is the great healer."

They excused themselves as a family came to talk to them, which was a good opportunity for Matthew to talk to Jack.

"Kids, go home and start lunch and I will join you in a while."

Hannah followed Jack's car and in ten minutes they were in front of a beautiful three-bedroom property. Jack opened the wooden gate and they parked their cars on the driveway.

The house had a paved front garden with a few pots of flowers at the side.

"My mum loved flowers," Jack said, "and I try my best to look after them. They remind me of her. You should see our back garden; it's pretty good. Sadly, I am not as good as she was."

He invited Hannah inside. On the left of the small hall was a little office, and on the right side was a large open-plan living room. On the right side was the kitchen, then the dining room, and on the left a large TV with a couch set.

"This is a very nice open house!"

"Yes, it's pretty good. We love it! Especially when we have friends for dinner."

"Thank you for inviting me here!"

"I am really glad you came. Please feel at home. Would you like a drink?"

"Just a glass of water, please." She looked around and then asked him whether could help with lunch.

"You are not here to work, so just relax."

"Please, I would like to help." She followed him to the kitchen.

"All right, you can make a salad."

The front door opened and Matthew came in.

"Oh, good, kids, you are here. I am starving!"

"Lunch is almost ready!" It was all set up in no time and they all sat down.

"Hannah, how are you? How is your family? Do you have any brothers or sisters?" asked Pastor Miller, wanting to start a conversation.

It was a question that no one had asked her in a long time, but this time, it was not painful for her to answer. Truly, her Lord had healed her over the years. The scars and memories and life lessons had brought her near to the Lord into an intimacy of love, knowledge and wisdom, into a deep revelation of his mercy, grace and goodness.

"No, sir." She paused, smiling sadly.

They both looked at her, not knowing what to say.

"My mum, her name was Anna, died when I was 16, and I was raised, in a way, by my brother John. He was 26 at the time, much older than me."

"So, you live with him?"

"No, he died a few years ago in a car crash. I could not save him. The Lord called him to heaven. It is just me. Me and my cat Benny and my friend Laura; we have been best friends for many years now. She is a pharmacist at the same hospital as me. We share a house. It's actually the house that my brother bought just before he died."

"You must have gone through a lot," Matthew said.

"Yes, but God was good to me. He looked after me and I could not have made it without Him. He brought me closer and closer and grace carried me through. Healing took time, but I am here by His grace and love and mercy."

Jack smiled sadly.

"We lost mum a few years ago, didn't we, Dad, and it was very hard for us, too, in a different way."

"Yes, son, it was, but now we are all here together. God is good."

"That is when I went astray with the wrong friends. It was so painful that I could not understand and did not know how to deal with it. And then it happened. The car crash was, for me, a wake-up call. And the Lord sent you, Hannah! You are my angel."

Hannah had heard Jack speaking before about the dark side of the past years; it was something he would not speak about much.

"I wish I could have been an angel for John, my brother, and my mum, as well." Then she added modestly, "Thank you, Jack. I am trying my best to do my job and help."

"Thanks, Hannah. I am just a patient you are visiting today. Makes me feel really good!"

Jack stood up from the dining table, feeling frustrated and offended. He could not even look at her. He went into the kitchen to make tea.

"I did not mean that. No, you are not just a patient."

There was tension in the air, so Matthew intervened and asked Hannah to come and sit on the couch to have a chat about the church.

"Hannah, what do you think about our church?"

"I really loved it today. Long ago, one of my friends invited me to a conference there. I actually go to a small Baptist church, but I keep thinking I should maybe go to a larger church."

"You can join us if you like it. Think about it."

"I will think about it. However, I work alternate weekends, which makes it hard for me to be there every Sunday, which I would love to do. I will pray first and see what the Lord says about it. The hospital has a lovely place where you can pray, and I often go there and find it very refreshing to sit quietly with the Lord."

"It would be great to have you there. What do you think, Jack?" Jack had gone quiet, which was normal behaviour for him when he was upset, hurt or frustrated. He wanted to really matter to Hannah, not be some patient that she looked after and then would never see again.

He went to sit next to his father on the couch.

"Yes, that would be great. Do you have any hobbies, Hannah?"

He was calm, which surprised Hannah but not his father, who knew him well. He was not a person to hold a grudge or be upset for a long time.

"I have few, but my favourite ones, when I have time, of course, are my little flower garden and reading."

Jack smiled.

"You like flowers like my mum. You could help us with our little garden here!"

Her phone started to ring and she apologised and answered.

"Hello, Dr Parson!"

She listened and then asked, "Was it the lungs collapsing?"

She listened a few more minutes and then added, "I understand. So the family was informed. All right. Ok. I will… Yes, of course. See you tomorrow."

When she hung up the phone, she was very quiet.

"We lost Rob today. A father of two little kids. He came in two days ago and he did not make it. Unit C is mostly emergencies and accidents, as you know. Not everyone makes it. We pray and hope."

Then she covered her face with her hands and started to cry gently. She always cried for each patient that she lost. It was a battle she lost on Earth, but the Lord was calling them to a better place. Well, she did not know that, but she hoped and prayed they would make it to heaven.

"I am so sorry, but it is always hard when we lose someone. My team knows me by now. I always cry. Each one of us is in God's hands, and we trust Him as He knows his best."

"Of course, Hannah!"

"Let's give her some time, son." Matthew walked to the kitchen and got busy, but Jack did not move.

Then unexpectedly, maybe even for him, he followed the music in his heart and went to sit next to her on the other couch. He wished he could take away her pain. Gently, he put his arms around her and held her tight.

"It's ok, I am saved," he whispered.

Hannah leaned her head on his chest and kept crying.

He could hear her heartbeats as she sat curled in his arms.

"Please don't cry. I don't like to see you sad."

Her tears were making his shirt wet, but he did not mind. He wanted to look after her and protect her, but he was not always the best with words. She realised that Jack had been holding her for a few minutes, and she lifted her head. Their eyes met.

"I am sorry!"

"Why?"

"I don't know. I am making a scene. I should go." She felt embarrassed.

He gently let go of her but kept holding her hand.

"When can I see you again?"

Hannah looked at him kindly but pleaded, "Jack, you need to give me time! This is too quick for me!"

"Is it, Hannah?"

He stood up, took a card from the table and gave it to her.

"If you miss me, call me." He looked at her with love.

Matthew smiled but said nothing except good bye and a few words to Hannah before she left.

Jack walked her to the car and opened the brown gate for her to get out. As she was about to get into the car, Jack said, "Hannah, thank you for coming today. Hope to see you again soon."

They stood still for a moment. Then she put her hands around his neck, gave him a kiss on the cheek and put her head on his chest.

"I will miss you, Jack."

He put his arms around her and whispered, "I will miss you more!"

With tears in her eyes, she drove off quickly.

When Jack returned to the house, Matthew smiled.

"What do you think about Hannah, son?"

"Amazing woman. Can you imagine her having such a hard life?

"Yes, she had a hard life. But she has a strong faith and a heart for the Lord as not many have."

"Do you think she will come again?"

"At church or to see you?"

"Both."

"Of course she will. You need to give her time, son. "

"Yes, yes, time. And I need to develop patience."

His father laughed as patience was not what Jack was best at.

"You are getting better at it, Jack. Now you know what to pray for: patience, son!"

At last, Jack felt he was on the right path in his life. The Lord was opening doors of favour, not only for church, work and friends, but for love. His heart was filled with music, and that was something he was eager to share with Hannah. She was making music to his heart, and he could hardly wait to meet her again.

That evening, his prayers were full of joy as he felt the Lord was directing his heart toward Hannah. She was more than he'd ever imagined. His dreams of meeting a woman who would really touch his heart had come true, and he did not know how to react or what to do. He felt overwhelmed by God's favour and grace; he had been given another chance when he knew he did not deserve it.

He felt he was not worthy of having such a delicate, beautiful and brave woman in his life. He felt honoured to see her and be with her; he was still thinking about how he'd held her in his arms. Yes, his father and Mike were right: he was in love.

And he wanted to follow his heart.

Chapter 8

Waiting

Hannah was back at work and back to her normal schedule. But something was different, and she wished Jack would call her. She was thinking of dropping him a message asking how he was but did not know how to do it. It was much easier to deal with hospital challenges than deciding what and when to write to Jack.

She finished her shift and was on the way home when around 6 pm she heard her phone beeping and received a message. She was surprised as was not expecting anyone to send her a message at this time. She looked and saw it was from Jack. When she got home, she was alone as Laura was out for the evening with her fiancé and it was just her and Benny.

John 10:27
My sheep hear my voice, and I know them, and they follow me.

She put the phone on the table and had a shower. When she came out of the shower, she looked again at the phone. She was thinking it might be a good idea to read the message but changed her mind, put the dinner on and turned on the TV. She found something to watch on Netflix and finally decided to read the message.

"Hi Hannah, I was thinking of you. How are you? Jack."

It was a very short message, shorter than she had expected. At least he had written something. She decided to answer, which was unusual for her as she always took her time unless it was an emergency. She mainly received phone calls and messages from the hospital, and most of her friends were working at the hospital.

"Hi Jack, I am fine thank you. Just finished work. I was thinking of you, too. Hannah."

A few minutes after she'd sent the message, the phone rang and it was Jack. Looking at the phone, she did not know what to do, but she did pick it up.

"Hello, Jack!"

"Hello, Hannah! How are you?"

"I am fine, thank you."

"I was thinking of calling you to see if you wanted to meet sometime this week. When you are free?"

"Yes, I could meet you Wednesday afternoon. I work till 5 pm."

She heard a happy voice on the other end of the phone.

"I will take you out for dinner! What time can I pick you up?"

"Let's say 6."

"Great! See you Wednesday."

Once she'd hung up the phone, she felt anxious. She was only going out with a friend. Hmm. However, Jack had become very dear to her heart, and if she kept meeting him, he might end up becoming more than a friend.

Wednesday came very quickly, and she put on something simple and was ready. Jack was not late. At 6 pm, he arrived with flowers. Laura opened the door.

"Hello, you must be Jack. I am Laura, Hannah's friend. I will tell her you're here."

"Nice to meet you, Laura. I will wait here."

When Hannah appeared, he gave her the flowers. She felt spoiled.

"You are always so sweet."

Jack smiled. "I try my best," he said, teasing her.

She asked Laura to put the flowers in a vase and went out with Jack.

***

When she sat next to me in the car, I felt so happy.

"I am surprised you are here!"

"Why?" she asked.

Looking again at her, I just added, "You look so beautiful!"

We drove to the restaurant, I parked the car and we went inside. It was a beautiful Italian restaurant. I had made a reservation, and we had a little round table at the back.

"So, Jack, I am here!"

"Yes, I thought you would be too busy to meet me, or you might have had a handsome guy already taking you out."

She looked at me and very seriously said, "No, I do not work all the time. As for dating, I have not done that for years. So, no. I do not have anyone in my life."

I did not know what to say or how to start the conversation.

"How was your week?"

"Fine, thank you. Hospitals are busy with emergencies. However, we had two patients who went home, which was very good. It encourages us, the nurses and the doctors, to see people healed and moving back to their lives."

A waiter brought some cold drinks for us.

"What about you, Jack?"

I smiled and shook my head.

"Since I am a manager, I have various responsibilities, and I am adapting to my new office and all the things I need to deal with. However, on the other side, I am also looking forward to working more and more with Mike on the project we are developing at church. You met Mike, did you?"

"No, I did not. But I would like to meet him. And yes, I heard about your project. It seems very complex."

"Yes, it is. If you want to and have time, I could share it with you."

She looked at me and paused.

"I might have a few hours over the weekend. As you know, I work shifts, and lately I have been helping in Unit B a lot. "

The food was served and we changed the subject.

"I've just read Psalm 37:4-5 and was thinking of the Lord fulfilling the desires of our hearts."

"I love that verse, Jack. It is one of my favourites. But my desires are few at the moment. I'm not sure I've made a list as some might."

"What are your heart's desires, Hannah?"

Surprised by the question, she made big eyes, paused and looked far away. "Not many; at this point, everything is somewhat limited for me. Maybe it is because I dream big for others. I'm not sure what to wish for myself, or rather, I've never thought about it much."

"Maybe you can start thinking of some new things – what do you say?"

"Yes, I am open to new ideas and new doors that the Lord opens, but each of us has our own passions and dreams. We have to work hand in hand with the Lord to be able to move on with the Lord in our lives."

"Of course, but if the Lord opens a door, He fills us with his grace and love and amazing things happen. Don't you think so?" I was not giving up leading the conversation.

She laughed and added, "You always challenge me, and the Lord through you, and I do love challenges!"

Gaining confidence, I took her hand in mine, and looking into her beautiful blue eyes, I said, "Now, I will challenge you! You are an amazing lady, beautiful, intelligent, fun…"

"Jack!"

"Wait, Hannah, I have not finished. I totally adore you and I've fallen in love with you. Would you do me the honour of being my girlfriend and going out with me?" Laughing, I added, "We are kind of going out now!"

Hannah looked slightly shocked.

"Are you serious, Jack?"

"Yes, I am more than serious. I have been thinking and praying, and now I finally have the courage to ask you out."

"Jack, I am honoured. I do not know what to say! However, I need some time to think about it and pray."

Jack felt disappointed and looked down.

"Please do not take it as a no. I love your company and love being with you, but dating, Jack, would involve a lot of change in my life and possibly yours. I need to make sure this is what my heart says, as well."

"All right, Hannah."

She looked at me and gently touched my cheek.

"I need to make sure my heart will not be broken as it was when I lost my mother and my brother. I do not want to get into a wrong relationship. You are so sweet. I love being with you. But I need time, please. I shall give you an answer in a couple of weeks."

We left the restaurant, and after parking the car on her driveway, I walked her to the door of her house.

"Goodnight, Hannah! It was lovely to be with you tonight and talk to you again."

"Goodnight, Jack. Thank you for the invite."

"I will wait to hear from you!"

***

As I opened the front door, Laura came straight to me.

"Well, did he ask you for a date?"

"Yes, he did! How did you know?"

She smiled and said confidently, "You can see from his eyes and behaviour that he is totally in love with you. So, did you say yes, Hannah?"

"No, actually, I did not say anything."

"What do you mean?"

I sat down on a chair, feeling tired and overwhelmed.

"I told him that I would give him an answer in two weeks."

Laura got upset and gave me a lecture.

"Sometimes I wonder what is wrong with you. He is an amazing man, and you know you are in love with him too. Why do you back off?"

"I am tired, Laura, and I want to go to bed. I need to make the right decision, and I will pray about it. Alright with you?"

The week passed quickly and my mind was on Jack. There was nothing from him on my phone; all my friends were texting, but not him.

I did want a break. But at the same time, I wanted to know how he was doing, and I was missing him.

On Sunday I decided to go to Northgate Church again. I had started going there regularly when I was not working, and I was looking forward to seeing Jack.

Sadly, that day, I did not see him and felt disappointed. Well, I was at church for the Lord, to worship and fellowship, but I had also been looking forward to meeting him again.

As the service ended, I stood up ready to leave. I spoke to a few ladies that I had made friends with over the past few weeks and then I saw him. He was standing in the front row, surrounded by a group of people, and there was a pretty young girl next to him. He turned around and our eyes met. For a moment, I felt time stood still. I lowered my eyes, turned around and slowly left.

He did not come after me, and I had to leave. I hoped he would come after me and talk to me, but he did not.

On the way home in the car, I had tears in my eyes. I really wanted to be with him but felt it would be quite a big change in my life, and I was afraid of a broken heart again. I was fighting with myself and with the Lord.

***

As our eyes met, I felt my heart beating fast. I really loved her and wanted to speak with her and tell her not to leave. But as she'd said she needed time, I did not want to push her into a relationship that she might not want. So even though my heart told me to move, for some reason I did not.

"Are you coming?" I heard Jessica saying to me in a loud voice.

"Yes, I am. Mike, are you coming too?"

"Wait, there are 10 of us going. I am trying to reserve a table for us at the Red Pub. What do you think?"

"Yes, fine with me!"

Chapter 9

The test of love

The weekend passed quickly. On Monday I had been invited by Mike to dinner, so I went and joined him and Patricia, his fiancée.

"Hey, Mike! Hey, Patricia!" I had brought a box of chocolates and a bottle of wine.

"You are always so nice to us." She gave me a polite hug and invited me in.

"How is work, Mike?"

"Oh, well, you know, we keep changing and building and making plans. I am working three hours from here this week, which is a bit challenging as I won't be able to be in my office and in the field as well. You know what it means to be a manager."

---

1 Peter 2:5
You yourselves like living stones are being built up as a spiritual house, to be a holy priesthood, to offer spiritual sacrifices acceptable to God through Jesus Christ.

I understood his situation and said calmly, "Yes, you are right. I do not like it when I am sent to look after other branches, but sometimes I have to do it; it is part of the job."

We all sat at the table, Patricia had cooked a very nice French dish and we had a good evening.

"Patricia and I were thinking that since we are getting married in a few months' time, we need a best man. Well, I do, so would you like to be my best man, Jack?"

I looked at him in surprise.

"Really? Yes, I know you are getting married. But me, are you sure?"

"We do look a bit like brothers," he said. "We have been best friends with ups and downs for years, no?"

"It would be an honour and my pleasure."

It made me so happy to be part of Mike's life; he was such a good friend and a very good man.

After dinner, we went into the little lounge and had a chat while Patricia was in the kitchen.

"Jack, tell me, what is going on in your life?"

"Nothing much, or too much, maybe!"

"I saw the way you looked at that girl on Sunday."

"What girl?"

"That girl at church with beautiful blonde hair. Are you in love with her?"

"Yes, that's Hannah. And yes, I am in love with her."

"Did you ask her for a date?"

I got up and walked around the room.

"Yes, I did, and we get along so well, but she …"

I felt sad and angry at the same time.

"She is always working; it's her hospital and her job, and she's always helping. She does not have time for me. I'm sure she will say no."

Mike, looking a bit confused, asked calmly, "I assume she did not give you an answer?"

"No, and I am tired, and I think I am giving up. She is wonderful, intelligent and beautiful, but I do not think I can do this, so it might be better for her to say no. I am not sure I have the patience anymore to keep waiting."

Mike put his hand on my shoulder.

"You should not give up. She must have some sort of feeling for you! Wait, pray and hope. Don't give up, Jack. It will be worth it! It will be alright; give her a chance!"

"You think it will be alright?"

"Yes. Did you send her a message?"

"Actually, I have run out of ideas about what to say to her! I wished on Sunday that she had not left."

"Did you try to speak to her yesterday?"

"True, true, Mike! I did not. I could not! I let her go."

"Send her a message. Just talk about life, your day. Ask her how she is, and leave it at that."

"All right, I might do that."

"Trust me, she will get back to you. She will know you are there for her. Just give her some time."

I took my friend's advice and did that, and she did answer my messages. But one day when I called her, something was wrong. The conversation was very short.

"Hello, Hannah. How are you? I have been thinking of giving you a call."

"Hello, Jack. I am very busy. I'm fine, thank you. Might see you Sunday at church."

***

On Sunday, I was not sure whether to go to church or not. Finally, I decided to go. I had tears in my eyes as I felt overwhelmed. It was so easy to work in a hospital, but this was something different. Something that I was doing for myself. It was my heart that was involved. I managed to calm down and look relaxed, even though my heart was still wandering and anxious.

As I entered the church building, I saw Jack. I felt so happy and wanted to talk to him but did not know what to do. Maybe he'd missed me and maybe we could meet sometime and finish our talk.

The service was about to start, and Jack was surrounded by lots of people. They seemed to be part of the morning team. Then next to him, I saw that girl, Jessica, and my heart sank. She gave him a hug and that was more than enough for me. I was not sure what to think and my mind stopped.

No one had seen me, and I turned around and left. I sat in my car and started to cry. And I kept crying all the way home. I felt I had lost Jack.

Laura had just got home from work. "What is wrong, girl? I don't see you cry often, only when a patient has died. Did someone die?"

"No, no. This is different."

She sat next to me on the couch.

"I thought you went to church?"

"Yes, and I came back."

"Why? What happened?"

"You were right. I should have said yes to Jack. Now, he has probably forgotten about me and will never ask me for a date again."

She looked at me in surprise and gave me a hug.

"Let me make you a nice hot chocolate and we will have a chat."

I was happy to cuddle under my blanket with my cat, and we had hot chocolate. I explained how I'd seen Jack with a girl and I could not stay in the church.

"You are in love, Hannah!"

I shook my head.

"Love is not what I am planning now. I am not sure I can go to that church now. It was really painful to see him with someone else!"

"You don't know; maybe she was just a friend. He is still sending you messages daily, and you still need to give him an answer."

"I am not sure I can say yes, anymore! I am in love and I miss him, but I feel so confused."

***

Later in the day, I received a text from Jack.

"Hello Hannah, are you ok? I was thinking of you as I did not see you at church today."

I did not answer. I was not in the mood to answer and I did not know what to answer.

The next day passed very quickly and I forgot to answer Jack, or rather, I just could not do it.

Driving home at 2 pm, I heard my phone ringing. I was not in the mood for Jack or anyone else.

As I was parking the car on the driveway, my phone rang again and I heard a voice on the other end.

"Hello, Hannah."

"Hello, Dr Bernstein."

"I was wondering if you could come earlier tomorrow as we might need some extra hands to help."

"Are you short-staffed?"

"No, but Unit B was asking whether you wanted to give them some help for an hour?"

"So they called you first? Hmm."

"They were a bit concerned that you might say no as they keep asking for your help."

"True, true, Dr Bernstein. Let me be nice. Tell them I can be there for morning rounds. What do you think?"

"That is very good of you. I will let you off around 2 pm, all right?"

"You always make sure I rest, don't you?"

"Hannah, you need to find yourself a nice man to look after you. I keep telling you that." Dr Bernstein spoke kindly.

At that moment, the phone rang and another call was on the line. Hannah apologised and answered.

"Hello, Hannah!"

"Hello, Jack!"

"How are you? I was wondering whether you wanted to go for a drink."

At this point, I was not in the mood for him or a chat. I had too much on my mind and was still feeling hurt.

"Really? Well, I'm not sure it is a good idea. You do have your life and friends and beautiful women around you. Why would you want to take *me* for a drink? Look, Jack, I am sorry, but I have to go. Goodbye." I was not angry, but I sounded upset, for sure. Once I'd hung up the phone, I started crying.

***

That evening was not the best evening for me, and my dad noticed and started to talk to me. Some conversations I did not want to have with my father or anyone. Not tonight, anyway!

"Jack, you seem upset."

"I am more than upset. I am angry!"

"Why? Someone at work gave you a hard time?"

"No, just Hannah. I asked her for a date a few weeks ago and she told me she would get back to me. I spoke with Mike and he told me not to give up on her. However, she did not even come to church as she had promised. Today she told me no, that she would not meet me. And that I have my friends and other women around me and effectively said goodbye. I felt so bad. Hurt and angry."

"Hmm… I can see you are angry."

"I do not know why I bother with her. I should forget about her."

"Really, son, so easily? Just because she did not answer your phone in time? Or because you had a little love quarrel or she was maybe tired and you caught her in a bad mood? You don't know, do you? Or maybe you are in a bad mood."

Jack looked at his dad and listened with interest, although he was not in the mood.

"Love, Jack, is not roses and sweet words; it is hard work and sweat and tears sometimes, and anger, sadly. In hard moments, you appreciate each other more and learn to say I am sorry! Try to give her a break and wait. I am sure she will come and speak to you. What do you think about inviting her to the party next Sunday in Rosie's memory?"

Jack was not sure he wanted to text her at all, but then he agreed with his father's suggestion.

"All right. I will wait one more day or so and then I will invite her, and if she says no, it is a no. But I am still angry with her."

"That's my boy. Trust me, she will say yes. And Jack, you need to pray and ask God to take your anger away."

Jack looked at his father and in a surrendered voice he said, "I am hurt, Dad. I am hurt. But I miss her." He smiled.

Chapter 10

Try again

After a couple of very busy days, lost in my work, I was thinking of Jack and of sending him a message. At that moment, I received a message from him.

"Hi Hannah, my father and I are doing a remembrance dinner with friends for my mum, Rosie. We would like to invite you to come on Sunday at 3 pm for a few hours. If you are busy, we understand, and we wish you all the best. Jack."

My heart melted, and I felt hope rising for another chance with Jack. I had felt bad for the past few days, and Laura insisted that I call him. Then she gave up on me and told me I needed to figure out what

Matthew 22:37-39
And he said to him, "You shall love the Lord your God with all your heart and with all your soul and with all your mind. This is the great and first commandment. And a second is like it: You shall love your neighbor as yourself."

I wanted. I already knew what I wanted, but I was afraid to walk on the path that the Lord had laid in front of me. Afraid to love, afraid to start something new, afraid of a relationship. The Lord was doing a new thing in my life, and I did not know how to handle it. I was praying, but prayers were much easier than actually walking on the path laid for me.

"Hi Jack, thank you for the invitation. I would love to come. Can I bring anything, like food?"

Immediately I received a text.

"Would you like me to pick you up at 2 from your house? And yes, you can bring anything you want! Thank you."

"Jack, I am working but should be home by then. I will bring something. Looking forward to seeing you at 2. Thank you. Hannah."

The rest of the week was quiet and neither of us dared to send any more texts. The good thing was I started to have a bit of hope that he was still in love with me and had not forgotten me. On the other hand, maybe it was just a polite invitation from his family in gratitude for being his nurse. However, I was praying a lot for him and my priorities were starting to change.

On Sunday I was working, but every five minutes I was looking anxiously at my watch.

At home, I told Laura that I was going to the memorial celebration for Rosie and she was so happy for me. Actually, she was happier than I was. I was not sure how I felt.

Before Jack pulled up in front of the house, I was pacing around and looked in the mirror 10 times. When I finally went out and saw him, he looked so handsome, dressed in a blue shirt with short sleeves and a pair of dark blue trousers. He smiled and was happy to see me, but he seemed to keep his distance. Maybe that was just my impression.

***

As we got into the car, I looked at her and she was beautiful. My heart still had music for her. Yes, love and love.

She had a lovely pink dress with blue flowers, and her hair was down on her shoulders. She looked like a princess.

I started talking to her about God, work, service at church, trying to bring her into the conversation, but she was very quiet. I tried to ask a lot of questions but got only short answers.

That did not make me give up; at least she was there.

She was looking out the window rather than at me, although I was trying my best. Then she said to me, "Can you stop the car please?"

I pulled to the side of the road as it was a quiet neighbourhood with nice houses and big oak trees.

"I can't do this!" she said. She got out of the car and started walking back.

I got out as well and did not know how to react, which was unusual for me. I went after her.

"Hannah, what is wrong?"

"Everything is wrong. I am sorry, I cannot do this."

I stepped quickly in front of her and she stopped. She lifted her head and looked straight into my eyes. Tears were running down her face like a river.

"I am overwhelmed, and it is too much for me. I don't even know what I am doing here."

I gently put my arms around her and held her tightly. She kept crying but she was holding me quite tightly.

After a few minutes, she raised her head and whispered, "Why are you here?"

"Do you really not know? Hannah, my father and I invited you to come for a day we celebrate to remember my mum, who was an amazing person. And I wanted you to come."

"Why, Jack? Why are you really here? Why would you call me?"

"Hannah, I want you to come..."

"Why would you call me, since you always have that girl with dark hair around you?"

I looked at her, confused. "Who?"

"She is always with you. So why would you want me?"

Even when she was crying, she looked beautiful.

Then I realised she was talking about Jessica.

"Oh, Jessica? She is my cousin! She is not my girlfriend, Hannah."

"She is not? But I saw her at church with you!"

"Hannah, she is not my girlfriend. Look at me, Hannah. Do you think I have a girlfriend? Jessica is my cousin."

Looking embarrassed, she said, "Yes, I even left church last week crying my eyes out! And the week before! Yes, I thought you had a girlfriend and had forgotten about me. She even gave you a hug."

Looking at her, I thought she was adorable and I was not angry with her. She made me smile.

"Oh, my little angel. So you *were* at church last week."

"I came, and when I saw you with her, I left. I did not even listen to the service. I wanted to see you, but I couldn't."

"Why didn't you come and talk to me?"

"Because I felt I had already lost you. And when I saw you two weeks ago, you did not even come and speak to me."

"True, Hannah. I honestly did not want to pressure you into a relationship and did not know what to do."

It was quiet for a moment and I could hear the music in my heart.

"Hannah Reynolds, I love you and I want to be with you. You are quite a challenge for me, but I love every bit of it!"

She looked at me seriously. "Jack, I love you too, and you are the best thing that has happened to me."

I took her in my arms and held her tightly. I could hear her crying and I could not let her go. She was so adorable and sweet, and I was her man.

"Hannah, Hannah!"

When she had calmed down, she said, "Did I make a fool of myself?"

"No, you probably just realised you are in love with me too."

She also realised they needed to go to Jack's house.

"Look at me! I am a mess. I cannot go to your house like this. I am sure there will be lots of people."

"At least a hundred. Let's walk a bit till you've calmed down and hope you don't cry anymore." I wiped her tears and looked into her beautiful eyes.

"Please do not cry! It's all good. And by the way, can we make it official that we are dating?"

"Of course. It's not a secret, is it?"

"The Lord is so good to me. Today is a beautiful day for me; I can't believe it." He laughed. "You thought I was dating Jessica! Adorable!"

"Stop it, Jack!"

We walked on in silence. I took her hand and she walked close to me.

"Jack, tell me I am not dreaming."

"If you are dreaming, I am dreaming too. And it is a beautiful dream."

A few minutes later, we drove home. Cars were parked along the entire street. The doors were open and we went in. As we walked toward the back garden, my dad began his usual speech, so we'd arrived just in time.

"Thank you all, friends and family, for coming today. It is a special day as Rosie went to be with the Lord. To us, it was a challenge as a family, but we had lovely, amazing friends supporting us: you.

Rosie was my wonderful, beautiful wife for many years, and I was blessed to have her in my life. So we invited you to celebrate Rosie's memory. Now, I will let Jack say a few words and we will have a prayer, and then we can all enjoy the lovely food and spend time with each other."

I went to the front and stood on the stairs near Dad.

"Mum was a lovely lady, and I was heartbroken when she left to be with the Lord, but I praise the Lord who gave us good friends and family to help us to get through this journey. She was an amazing mum, very kind and gentle and fun to be with. And, for sure, more patient than me."

Everyone laughed and I carried on.

"Today is a special day for me for two reasons: first as we are gathered here to remember her and pray, but secondly, I have been blessed and …" I stretched out my hand toward Hannah. She walked up to me, smiling.

"...the Lord has given me a beautiful, amazing woman in my life. This is Hannah, my girlfriend."

Everyone clapped happily.

We had a prayer and then Mike came to me.

"Jack, you did not tell me she was your girlfriend!"

"Well, we've just sorted things out today, so yes, since today."

I took Hannah by the hand and introduced them.

"Hannah, this is Mike, my best friend for so many years. He has put up with me for a long time. And this is Patricia, his fiancée."

"Hello, nice to meet you," said Hannah.

"So, you are the beautiful lady that stole his heart?" asked Patricia.

"She is my amazing angel, and I am truly blessed."

Chapter 11

Stand by me!

The day after that lovely Sunday afternoon, Hannah was again busy at the hospital. However, something had changed. Her life had changed, and her work was still a priority but in a different way. She was wondering whether he would call her. He did and left a message on her phone, but her phone was turned off at the time.

When she told Laura, she laughed.

"Hannah, I believe you are totally in love!"

"Yes, I am. I must be crazy to date him."

"Love is beautiful and mysterious, girl."

Hannah looked at her as she dried her hair after coming out of the shower.

Matthew 7:13-14

Enter by the narrow gate. For the gate is wide and the way is easy that leads to destruction, and those who enter by it are many. For the gate is narrow and the way is hard that leads to life, and those who find it are few.

"I've just come from work and I am tired. I want to eat and watch a movie and go to bed. I don't want you to lecture me about love."

Laura pushed the question.

"Stop worrying about the dinner and finding excuses. I know you. You keep working and working. I am really proud of you for actually finding a very handsome, amazing, Christian man."

"Yes, he is incredible."

She felt frustrated as her friend was not giving her a break.

"Do you miss him? Do you think of him?"

Hannah threw a pillow at her and went into the kitchen, but Laura followed:

"Leave me alone!"

"I won't. Answer me, Hannah. Be truthful to yourself. Do you miss him?" She laughed.

Hannah looked at her and took a big deep breath.

"He does have beautiful eyes and he is kind and very intelligent and so much fun to be with. Yes, I do miss him. We're dating. I would not date him if I were not in love, would I?"

***

Yes, Pastor Miller was right. I had been through a lot in my life and was now on a new road, gaining my trust back slowly.

I was pretty settled in my life, with my work and my cat and my little shared house and did not want any change or challenge. My work was challenging enough every day, and I loved my work.

But starting a relationship with Jack was a blessing. It was so much fun to be with him. He always challenged me, and we had so many conversations about God.

Yes, he was tall, blonde, blue-eyed, athletic, with an interesting life. He worked in a bank and was involved in church. Me – I was just a nurse. But I knew it would not be sweet and lovely all the time. We had already had some arguments and misunderstandings, but we were walking the path of love together.

I got home late, feeling tired. It was already 5 pm and I had not heard from Jack at all. My shift should have finished at 2 pm, but I stayed late.

I missed him and wished I could have spoken to him. The moment I sat on the couch to chill for a few minutes after my quick shower, I heard my phone ringing. It was a video call.

"Hi, Hannah. How are you?"

"Hi, Jack. So good to hear you."

He laughed and I could see him moving around in his kitchen.

"I am cooking dinner. I just got home and Dad is not home yet."

I realized I was in my pyjamas and bathrobe.

"Sorry, I am dressed for bed. I am in my pyjamas."

He looked at me and added, so genuinely, "You look beautiful, I can assure you. I had a busy day today, so I did not have time to send you a message, but what do you think about coming over for dinner tomorrow evening?"

"Yes, I would love that. Thank you. How is your dad?"

"He is fine. He had a busy day at church and stayed late. How is Dr Parson? And how was your work today?"

"Very good. We had five people coming through Emergency, and two went home. Dr Parson is fine. He's always at the hospital, more than at his home."

Jack stopped cooking for a moment.

"You look a bit tired, my pretty one. I'd better let you go to bed. And I see you have Benny cuddling you. Makes me a bit jealous."

"Yes, he follows me everywhere. You are right. I am tired, so I will eat something and go to bed. Your food looks good."

"Tonight, some pasta and chicken. There you go." He showed me the dish.

"My dad has just come in. I will have to go. Goodnight, my angel."

I had an early night. I was having to adjust to the idea I was dating. It was something unexpected and something beautiful, and I looked forward to walking this journey with Jack. I knew it would not be easy, but I was happy to give it a go.

Something very unexpected happened on Tuesday.

One of the nurses called me to tell me someone was looking for me. I thought it was a relative of a patient, and as I was about to start my rounds, I went toward the little office area.

I saw a very handsome man walking toward me. He was wearing nice trousers, a very nice light blue shirt and a big smile. It was Jack. He was holding a beautiful bouquet of red roses.

"Hi, Hannah!" He came closer and gave me a kiss on the cheek.

"These are for you because you are so beautiful and special!"

A few nurses passing by saw the flowers and started to giggle.

I did not know how to react.

"Thank you, Jack."

My heart filled with love.

"I do not know what to say!"

"Enjoy your work. See you tonight, at 6 pm. I just wanted to see you. I missed you."

"Thank you for the flowers." I took them in my arms and smiled.

The emergency bell rang crazily.

"That's me going!"

Then I did not know how to say goodbye.

"Can I get a hug?"

"You have to ask? Come here, my angel."

He hugged me and held me for a while until I heard a voice behind us.

"Hannah, we need you!" It was Dr Bernstein striding by.

"Go, go!" he said. I put the flowers in my office and ran off.

He watched me down the corridor and then he left.

All my colleagues were really impressed.

"Handsome guy! And lovely flowers, Hannah!"

"Yes... thank you!" I did not want to enter into conversation or details.

The day passed quickly and I was soon at Jack's house. He opened the front door for me.

"Hi, Hannah. Glad you are here. It's just us. Dad had a dinner engagement." He invited me in and the dining table was beautifully decorated.

"You did very well. It's impressive."

"Trying my best!" He smiled. "The food is almost ready. I baked something special. I hope you will like it.

"It smells delicious."

He asked me to sit on the couch and he sat next to me. He looked into my eyes for a moment and I felt embarrassed.

"Yes...?"

"Can I not look at you? I am trying to discover my girlfriend and learn about you."

"That is true. There is a journey of learning about each other. I am not sure I have such an interesting life as yours."

"Come on, Hannah. I could not do your job. You are amazing; all the hospital talks about you. I am so proud of you, do you know that?"

We had a lovely evening together and I felt something changing in my heart. I had been stretched and challenged lately, and it had not been easy, but it was a beautiful journey.

***

I had Friday and Saturday off.

What a lovely day I had on Friday. I did a little shopping and then spent some time in my garden, looking after my flowers. The sun was shining, and I started reading a book I'd purchased. It was about adventure and love and, of course, above all, about God.

Laura was working, and I was home alone with Benny. He came and curled up next to me on the little bench in my little garden, and we had a peaceful, relaxing time.

I was hoping to meet Jack over the weekend, but I received a phone call from the hospital and I took on an extra shift as they needed some help.

I forgot all about Jack and missed a few phone calls. When I returned from work, I found a message from Jack that he had been expecting me for lunch.

I had to call him back late on Saturday.

"Hi. Jack. I am sorry, I was working today and I forgot that we were supposed to meet for lunch. Look, I am working tomorrow, as they needed extra help. Shall I meet you next week?"

"Hannah, it's not the first time you have cancelled our dates and lunches. It seems to me you are too busy to have time for us, for me!"

"Jack, they really needed me at the hospital!"

"Are you the only one working there? Are you? Or don't you realise that I need you too?"

"Jack, I don't like the way you're speaking to me or the tone of your voice. I am trying my best at the hospital and with you, and..."

"Make up your mind, Hannah. If you put me on a schedule and your work comes before our relationship, then there is no point in continuing, is there? You obviously don't have time for me at all. Or only conditional time? Think about it. I am not happy with you at all. Goodbye."

In the quietness of the room, I started crying. I did want to do a good job at the hospital and I did want to be with Jack, and yes, I was working too much.

He was right in what he had said.

I could not pray much. I was tired and went to bed. Tomorrow was another day.

Sunday passed slowly at work. No one noticed I was sad as I was pretty good at hiding my emotions.

The moment I got home, I leaned against the door and fell on the floor, crying.

Laura was home and heard me.

"What is wrong with my girl? Are you alright?"

I could not say much and she helped me into the kitchen and made me a hot drink. I needed some company. I felt so lonely and miserable.

"I blew it, Laura, I did."

Laura took a chair next to me.

"First, have a shower. I will cook a nice dinner and then we'll talk; what do you say?"

Fifteen minutes later, we were enjoying a lovely dinner. I was calm and was able to explain my mess.

"I picked up too much work at the hospital and did not meet Jack yesterday. And we had an argument over the phone. Pretty short, I would say."

"Oh, my girl, listen, those things happen. But yes, you are working too much."

I looked at her with tears in my eyes.

"He was right. I do work too much and I have not had time for him for the past few weeks since we started dating. I've cancelled or missed many of our dates."

Laura gave me a hug.

"It will be alright. Did you pray about it?"

She was right. I did pray about it, and I did want to speak to him. However, I did not have the courage to call him.

***

On Monday morning, I was very determined when I spoke with Dr Bernstein.

"I have been thinking of my working hours, Dr Bernstein. I believe it would be best for me to stick with five shifts a week from now on. As you know, I've always picked up extra work, and I've done long shifts for many years."

Dr Bernstein closed the door of his office.

"Tell me, are you okay?"

"Yes, I am. However, I will never be able to have a life if I am always at the hospital. And even though I admire you and Dr Parson, I do not want to end up like him, making my home here."

Dr Bernstein smiled.

"Yes, you have started to date, haven't you? Hmm. Yes, I think your priorities are changing a bit, and your heart too. Am I right, Hannah?"

"Yes, you are right."

At home I prayed, and after a few more days, I decided, as prompted by the Lord, to send a text message to Jack.

"Hi Jack, I am so sorry for last week. I would like us to meet and talk. Can we meet tomorrow, since it is Saturday? Are you free? Hannah."

For some time, there was no answer. Maybe he was still upset with me or had moved on and we were no longer dating. I had all kinds of thoughts coming into my mind, but I was not willing to give up.

Around 7 pm, while I was on the couch watching TV, I heard the phone buzz and I received a message. It was from Jack.

"Hi Hannah, Yes, I would love to meet you. Shall we have a walk tomorrow around 3 pm and have dinner together? Greenland Park? Jack."

I had tears of joy in my eyes. Maybe he was not upset with me anymore and maybe all was good.

I stayed up late with Benny and enjoyed praying and relaxing and watching Netflix.

I asked the Lord, "Shall I go out tomorrow?"

And yes was the answer. The Holy Spirit prompted me to go and meet Jack. When you follow what the Lord says, he will open the right doors for you and amazing things will happen in your heart and your life.

Laura was right. I had not been on a date since my brother died, and that was more than a few years ago. Now I was adapting and reorganising my life, and it was harder than I thought.

The Lord was stretching me in an area where my heart seemed frozen. I had been waiting for love and a new beginning but had never tried and never said yes so far. And more importantly, I had not found a true heart match like Jack before.

Laura came home tired from work; we had a little chat and she encouraged me regarding meeting Jack. She promised to help me choose my clothes as she had a day off and would be home.

Chapter 12

Where are you?

On Saturday we both had a lie-in, and then around 12, I knocked on her door.

"Yes! Come in, Hannah! Are you anxious about going out and meeting Jack? Come on, girl, I will help you choose something simple and nice. I am sure he has forgotten he was upset with you."

"You think so? I am just going for a walk and dinner."

"Of course; he is in love with you. My dear Hannah, sometimes I wonder what planet you're on. I keep telling you that you are working too much and you get disconnected from the world."

Hebrews 4:12

For the word of God is living and active, sharper than any two-edged sword, piercing to the division of soul and of spirit, of joints and of marrow, and discerning the thoughts and intentions of the heart.

She picked out a nice pink t-shirt with a floral design, then found a beautiful short-sleeved shirt with a blue rose in the middle.

"What do you think?"

"I prefer the t-shirt, honestly. Why not?"

When it was time to go, Laura was more anxious than I was. She gave me a hug.

"You look so…"

"Pink!" I laughed.

"No, adorable. My lovely Hannah, ready to go out. I am so happy for you. Have a blessed time and let me know how it goes."

"I think I am crazy to go and meet him."

I felt that my heart was rushing ahead of me, but once I started to walk, I enjoyed the good weather and the birds, trees and people. It was quite a walk to the park, like 30 minutes, but that did not bother me. It was a beautiful park, and I went there every couple of weeks when I had time.

It was lovely to sit on a bench in the summer and read and listen to the birds. It was a big, well-developed park. My favourite section had flower beds and lovely quiet walks. I was looking forward to walking there with Jack.

There were a few crossings on the way, and as I was waiting at one to cross, a car approached at speed, went into a skid and spun around. I reacted quickly and pushed a nearby lady out of the way.

At that moment, I heard a thud, felt pain and was knocked to the ground.

***

On the other side of the park, Jack was waiting. And waiting. He decided to sit on a bench and started reading something on his phone. After 20 minutes, he looked worriedly at his watch. After 10 more minutes, he called Matthew.

"Hey Dad, it's me... Did Hannah call you by any chance? She has not come and she is already 30 minutes late!"

"No, she didn't. Wait a little longer and see; she might come."

"All right, but I have not known her to be late."

I waited some more and then at 4 pm I called Dad again.

"Hey Dad, shall I meet you at the Italian restaurant since Hannah did not come? I have a reservation, so I will take you for dinner."

"Why not? I will let you pay the bill, son," he said with a laugh.

We met 30 minutes later at the restaurant and had a pleasant time together.

"I am a bit upset again, Dad. Or more than a bit!"

"Why, son?"

"Hannah did not come, and I wanted so much to see her. We had an argument last week, and I could not call her or text her. Each day I wanted to contact her, but I couldn't. Then yesterday she sent me a beautiful text saying sorry and asking to meet me today."

"Maybe something came up and she could not come."

"I am afraid she is too involved in her world, with work and her hospital friends, and she might be working again."

"Jack, you are a very nice young man. Before you go with "what if", I believe it is best to pray and wait and not make judgements till you find out the truth."

The rest of the evening they talked about the Give Hope project.

"How is the project going, Jack?"

"Pretty well. I spoke with Mike and we're getting organised slowly. We are using the big office on the right for setting up. As you know, we rented the warehouse near to the church and we'll see how we can organise it into categories: food, clothes, objects, etc. We have Claire making the phone calls and setting things up with companies, charities and whoever wants to help with donations or is needing support. It is quite complex. We have 10 volunteers a day now, and things are moving. In a couple of weeks, we hope to open and have a schedule. Each family will come and fill in a form, and we will be able to look after their needs. I would also like to set up financial support for them, such as vouchers; Mike and I have discussed it. We will have to talk to the leaders of the church and inform you all…"

Jack's phone rang and he picked it up.

"If it is from the hospital, Jack, I hope is not someone in the church who is sick or I'll have to leave," whispered his dad.

"Hello, Laura."

"Hi, Jack. I am so sorry to bother you. I am at the hospital. Hannah was hit by a car this afternoon. She was on her way to meet you, Jack."

"I'm coming right away."

"I will have to talk to the doctors; I'm not sure they will let you in. It depends on her condition. I've just found out!"

"Trust me, they will let me in, Laura. I will be there soon."

"Is everything all right?" asked his dad.

"Hannah is in hospital! She was hit by a car. I am going there now."

"I guess I will pay the bill and then I will be on my way home. I will pray for you both. Jack, call me when you know something."

"Thank you, Dad, and you were right. I should not have jumped to conclusions."

***

As I left for the Green Bell Hospital, I was not sure how welcome I would be. The important thing for me was that she was on the way to meet me. I did not like the fact that she was probably injured in the accident, and I didn't know her condition. That did worry me! And we'd had an argument the previous week and things were a bit in the air between us.

I did speak rather harshly to her and I was angry, but on the other hand, I did not want to come second after her job; some balance and stability would be good in our lives. Some people are workaholics and obsessed with their work; others are obsessed with friends or too much sport. Each of us, sooner or later, becomes distracted from the path laid by the Lord. Then all kinds of troubles and hardships confront us, and getting back on the right track gets harder.

As soon as I asked at reception for Unit C, Dr Parson, I was invited upstairs. That surprised me as I thought I would have to justify why they should let me in.

It was after 7 pm and Dr Parson was not very busy.

"Hello, Jack. Don't worry, we do allow family visits late; we are an emergency unit. And now Hannah is here again."

"Thank you."

He walked with me to her room.

"Now, Jack, don't worry; she is not too bad. But I need you to know she is a lovely lady. She must care a lot for you as she cut down her work hours last week, which surprised both me and Dr Bernstein. But we were happy about it as we knew you two were dating. She does need someone to look after her as she looks after everyone. Jack, I hope you will look after her."

"Yes, I am, Dr Parson. By the way, I did not know she had cut down her work hours."

"Yes, she did. She had been planning this for a long time but confirmed it last week."

Outside her room, he whispered, "Our Hannah is a little hero. A car lost control near Greenland Park, and Hannah saved the life of a lady by pushing her out of the way. She was hit by the car instead. An amazing story, if you hear it in detail. It might even be in the newspapers by Monday."

He was talking a bit too much; I was impatient to see her.

"And how is she?"

"Well, sleeping. She was hit on the left side again. We need to take more tests tomorrow. It might not be a nice view, but do not worry. She will be fine."

As I went in, it was not a nice view, as Dr Parson had said.

Her beautiful face was bruised and her left arm bandaged.

"Hannah, my angel. Hannah!"

I sat down next to her on a chair, held her hand and took a deep breath.

"I am here, Hannah. It is me, Jack."

She did not answer and I assumed she was asleep.

"I am sorry about last week. Please forgive me for the words I said. I did not want to hurt you. I was selfish and angry."

I gently touched her face and wished she was awake. As it was very quiet in the room, I added, "I wish you were at home with me, not here."

I put my head on her hand, and she suddenly moved and spoke.

"Hey, Jack!" She opened her eyes.

"Hannah!"

"I am the one to say I am sorry. You were right: I was working too much!" Then she closed her eyes.

"Are you all right?"

Then she had convulsions but managed to press the emergency bell. She was coughing up blood, and I did not know what to do.

"I am sick... leave, Jack...!"

Dr Parson swept into the room.

"Jack, I am afraid you'll have to wait outside, please!"

"Hannah, you need to calm down!"

To the nurses, he said, "She might have internal injuries. We need to see what is causing the bleeding; otherwise she might lose too much blood."

Once Hannah had stopped shaking, she said slowly, "I think my ribs are broken!"

Dr Parson laughed.

"Will you stop being a nurse? You are the patient! But you are right; I think you have a few ribs broken. We'll do some tests tomorrow. Dr Bernstein will be with you, all right, girl? Now, sleep."

"Jack!"

"All right. Three minutes only, you understand!"

"Thank you!" She nodded.

***

Jack went into a small waiting room and called Matthew, who was waiting to hear some news.

"Dad, it's me. Hannah is injured quite badly. Her left side is bandaged and she is all bruised. She is not looking good. I am concerned. I will see if I can see her for five more minutes before I leave, and then I'll let her rest. I hope to get home by 9."

"Jack, do not worry. The Lord is with her. And we are praying. I'll ask for prayers for her tomorrow at church as well."

Those five extra minutes in Hannah's room were very hard for Jack.

"Hannah, I will come and see you tomorrow. I just want you to know I love you and I am praying for you."

He gave her a kiss on the cheek and held her hand for a moment. She was already asleep and did not even hear what he said. Dr Parson came back into the room.

"Jack, she probably has some ribs broken. We'll know more tomorrow as we have to do a lot of tests. Go home and rest. We are looking after her. Don't worry."

Jack could not remember how he got home. He felt really tired.

"I feel bad, Dad, and I wish I could do something!"

"You cannot do anything, son, for now. Just pray."

"I think I will go upstairs to my room and spend some time with the Lord."

A few minutes later Matthew heard him playing his guitar. Many mixed feelings invaded Jack's heart. He had not even met up with her, and now she was in hospital. She was bruised, but at least she was not in a coma. He knew about accidents, and she knew even more, working in Unit C.

It was good to see her, and she had even said sorry. That was so sweet of her when he was the one making assumptions and getting angry.

He could not sleep and prayed many times. He asked the Lord to save Hannah, heal her, and help her through the night. He asked the Lord for a chance to see her, to be with her.

In the end, he went downstairs, had a cup of tea, turned on the TV and watched something funny for 30 minutes.

Matthew came downstairs as he heard the noise.

"You cannot sleep, son?"

"No, Dad. I prayed and now I cannot sleep."

"Are you thinking of Hannah?"

"Yes. I wish I knew more about how she is. Do you think I can go and see her tomorrow, again? I want to see her. She needs to know I am there for her."

Matthew gave his son a much-needed hug.

"Jack, you need to trust the Lord and wait. The Lord works all things for the good of those who love Him. It's good to spend time with the Lord. Sometimes we forget to let him take care of our loved ones in moments like this. The Lord will do a better job than you. Trust me, He knows how to look after Hannah."

"Yes, you are right, Dad. You are right."

The Lord is a good Father, and Jack knew that. He had carried him through a lot of things, even when he fought with the Lord. He had never left him and had poured out His grace.

Yes, Jack knew what it meant to trust the Lord, lean on him and let Him work his will.

His plan was always the best and His will was always perfect, filled with love and truth. God always made a way.

By surrendering and leaving it all at Jesus' feet, Jack always moved forward.

Chapter 13

Trust and wait

The morning finally came and they both went to church. Matthew preached a very good sermon. Jack, on the other hand, found it hard to be there; he was part of the Start team, and he was doing the program for introductions that Sunday.

His dad told him he'd done a good job, but he didn't really believe him.

At the end of the service, it was prayer time and one of the ladies asked to speak as she wanted the church to pray for something special. And after that, Matthew was going to ask for prayers for Hannah. Jack had told him he could not do it as it was too much for him emotionally.

Matthew 17:20
He said to them, "Because of your little faith. For truly, I say to you, if you have faith like a grain of mustard seed, you will say to this mountain, 'Move from here to there,' and it will move, and nothing will be impossible for you."

The lady was pregnant and a bit shy, but she dared to speak.

"Hello, I am Mary. The Lord granted me grace and protection yesterday, and I want to share with you something amazing that happened to me. As you can see and many know, I am six months pregnant and expecting a baby girl. Yesterday, in the centre of town, near Greenland Park, I was waiting for a crosswalk. A car lost control in the middle of the road and spun around. At that moment, as in a dream, a young girl pushed me out of the way. It happened so quickly that I did not have time to react. I fell down and then I heard a bang. Now, it is a miracle I am here. I would probably have been hit. Praise the Lord for his protection."

The young lady had tears in her eyes.

"I felt I was protected by an angel. That girl was my angel. She is in hospital and I don't know anything except that her name is Hannah. I would like to pray for her as if it had not been for her, I and my baby might not have been here today. Thank you."

Jack and his dad looked at each other. They knew the entire story now. Pastor Matthew asked her to stay on the stage and he came up.

"I can confirm that, yes, she is Hannah Reynolds. My son, Jack, and Hannah are dating. The doctors and nurses do call her "the angel" of the Green Bell

Hospital where she works as a senior nurse. God is doing amazing things through that young lady. We found out last night that she is in hospital, in the emergency unit."

All the church stood up and prayed for Hannah and the doctors and nurses at Green Bell Hospital.

Jack was so touched that he was speechless. He was waiting for the service to finish and to go and see Hannah as he had been granted 10 minutes by Dr Parson.

On the way to the hospital, Jack said to his father, "Stop the car. I cannot go, Dad. I cannot go to see Hannah."

His dad pulled over on the side of the road.

"Jack, we were granted a short visit at 2 pm, and it would be good to go."

"I am not sure I can see her like this, as a patient, injured and bruised. It's too much for me. I don't want to lose her, Dad."

"Son, let's go and not make plans. Let's see what the Lord says and does, and we'll let the Lord lead us and teach us. She is in God's hands. He is looking after her."

Jack said nothing till they reached the hospital.

They went up to Unit C, but now it was different. Jack still felt anxious, on one hand not wanting to see her, and on the other hand, wanting to be there for her.

"Dr Bernstein!"

"Jack, Matthew, so nice to see you. And you're looking so good, young man. You are doing great. Your report says you healed marvellously, and I am impressed."

"How is Hannah?" asked Jack, "May we see her?"

"Hannah is an exceptional young lady. However, she has been hurt, mostly on her left side. You know that as you came yesterday, Jack. Now, I can let you in for only 10 minutes. I think it would be best for just one of you to go in. I guess Jack." He smiled at him.

Jack tried to smile but still looked concerned.

"Dr Bernstein, how is she really doing?"

"At this point, her left side is all bandaged and bruised. We're hoping she will not have a temperature again as that would mean an infection and we would need to give her more antibiotics. The scan showed that she has a few ribs broken. Otherwise, she is sleeping a lot."

"The lady that she saved attends our church and she is pregnant. You could say that Hannah saved two lives," Matthew was proud to add.

"Amazing girl, amazing. I've heard the story."

He opened the door and entered. Matthew stayed outside, just getting a peek, and Jack was the one who entered.

"I've heard that you're the one she is dating. You must be really happy. She is such a lovely girl.

That is our Hannah, always looking after all of the patients and nurses, working in all units and never complaining." The doctor left.

Jack looked at her and his face betrayed a pain that came from his heart. He went near the bed and looked at all the drips she was on and her arm all bandaged up.

"Hello, Hannah! It's Jack."

She did not react at all, but he carried on talking in a soft voice.

"I've heard you have been such a brave woman. Well done! We are all proud of you for saving a mother and her baby."

He moved closer and held her right hand. She had such delicate, small hands.

"You are so beautiful! I am so happy to see you."

He did not know what else to say. He closed his eyes, took a deep breath and said a prayer for her.

Her hand moved in his hand and she opened her eyes.

"Jack!" she whispered.

He made a sign for her not to talk.

"I am here. I've come for you."

"Jack, I am tired!" she said and closed her eyes.

He kissed her hand and held it tightly.

"Hannah, you make music to my heart."

She did not answer and seemed to be asleep.

The door opened and a nurse told him that his time was up. He had no choice but to leave.

On the way home, his dad asked him how she was.

"She actually said my name. She looks beautiful. But she was mostly asleep. You had a glimpse of her. She is really…"

"Bruised and bandaged."

"Yes, you could say that."

"Do you plan to see her again soon?"

"Yes, I would like to go each day, even if I am allowed only 10 minutes."

The evening passed quietly and Matthew noticed how sad Jack was.

"You are very quiet, Jack!"

"Yes, I am. Maybe too quiet. My heart goes out to Hannah, and it is too much for me at the moment. I love her and I do not want to lose her like we lost Mum. I want the Lord to give me a chance to bring Hannah back into my life to continue where we left off. I do not deserve such an angel as her, but I want to try my best and be there for her."

"Oh, Jack, let's take a day at a time and see how she improves. Only the Lord knows when it's our time to go to heaven. I am praying for the Lord to heal her. You two are young and have your lives ahead of you. Do not worry."

The next day, Jack called the hospital after work to ask how Hannah was and whether he could visit for 10 minutes or so.

Dr Bernstein answered.

"Hello, Jack. How are you?"

"Very well, thank you."

"How can I help you?"

"I called to inquire about Hannah and whether I could possibly visit her."

"I am sorry, but today we are not allowing visits to her room as she got worse, sadly. She has a bad infection in her arm and she is on medication to reduce the temperature and swelling. She took a really bad hit and it will take her time to recover. Why don't you give me a call tomorrow and see how she is and maybe you can come tomorrow?"

"Thank you, I shall do so," said Jack.

He felt a bit disappointed and decided to spend his afternoon at home. He went into the back garden and his father found him reading and meditating.

The next day, he was told he could not go to the hospital for a week. Eventually, his prayers were answered when he called and they told him, "Hannah is better. She ate a bit today and she is not sleeping so much. Would you like to visit her?"

He was so happy that he called his father, who was alarmed to get a phone call in the middle of the day.

"Hello, Dad."

"Hello, Jack. Is everything all right?"

"Yes, I just called the hospital and they're letting me see Hannah. I am so happy. I will see you later."

He hung up and rushed to the hospital. He did not have time to go home; he went straight from work, dressed in his dark trousers and a white shirt. He bought a beautiful bouquet of pink roses and looked very smart. When he walked into the hall, he felt confident and hope rose in his heart.

As he entered Unit C, one of the nurses told him to wait as she was making a phone call. Sometimes they communicated by phone as it was quite a long unit with lots of rooms and space for many people.

Once he heard he could go, he walked through the hall with a joyful heart. When he opened the door, she was in her bed, but she was not asleep.

"Hello, Hannah!"

Looking at him in surprise, she smiled. Her eyes looked tired but beautiful, and she was not sure how to react to seeing Jack.

She had slept a lot lately and had not worried about everything that had happened in the past week or so.

"Hello, Jack."

He gave her the flowers and then found a vase and put them in water for her.

"Thank you for the flowers. You know I love flowers."

He sat next to her on the bed and looked at her.

She felt shy, and he spoke kindly to her.

"I've been looking forward to seeing you. They didn't let me see you the past few days."

"Yes, I was not very well."

Their eyes met and he smiled and touched her hair and gave her a hug.

"I have missed you, Hannah."

She did not know what to say. Fear and doubt came into her heart, but she heard that music again: love that was pushing away all the doubts.

"I am so sorry for last week. You were right. I was working too much. I cut down my working hours to five shifts a week and I'm not picking up extras. And yes, I will try my best not to forget to meet you." He smiled and said nothing. "You know, Jack, this is quite a change for me as I honestly did not plan to have a relationship and to fall in love."

He took her hand in his.

"Hannah, since nothing is simple with you and me, I want to say a few things to you. I am so sorry. I was angry and said things that hurt you. You are in my heart. You are an amazing, wonderful woman and so beautiful and intelligent. And your love and passion for the Lord and ability to impart grace are amazing. I've never met anyone like you in my life. However, we both need to adjust, and sometimes we will have quarrels. But I am not planning to leave you. I love you."

"You are incredible, Jack, you know."

She heard the Lord speaking to her heart and took a deep breath. She withdrew her hand from his and started to cry.

"I am overwhelmed!"

He smiled and said, "No problem. I can give you as many hugs as you want." He was teasing her and gave her a hug.

"Why are you so good to me?"

"Because I made a decision to stand by you no matter what, and you're the best thing that has happened in my life after giving my life to the Lord! So, now I want to look after you."

She felt tired and wanted to sleep.

"Please let me take care of you."

She nodded off as he started to read from the Bible, John 19.

He gave her a kiss on the cheek, pulled up the covers, left the Bible next to her and quietly left the room.

***

"All good with you two?" my father asked on the way home.

"Yes, Dad, I think I am learning how to look after myself and my girlfriend. Or I am getting better at it. You know: communication, truth and love are very important, and yes, God's grace. The Lord is good to me. She was so kind to me, and she was the first to say sorry. It was, in a way, both our faults. We are learning to adjust our lives, and it is not easy."

"No, it is not. Your mum was always the most patient. But she used to have a go at me sometimes, especially if I was late. When you get angry, you are so much like her."

"I guess I am learning patience slowly, Dad."

"Any plans for visiting her tomorrow?"

"Yes, of course."

I felt so blessed and honoured to date Hannah. I was not sure about many things, but bringing all things to the Lord in prayer made me feel humbled, and I knew that the Lord, as always, was giving me wisdom. He was helping me and guiding me, showing me how to become more and more like Him, filled more and more with his Spirit and grace. God was so good. So, so good. His blessings were amazing, and my desire was to fulfil his will.

I had just learned one of the first lessons in my relationship, and that was good communication and an open heart filled with love and grace.

The next day when I went to see Hannah, she was doing better.

"Hi, Jack. How are you?"

"I am fine, thank you. How are you doing?"

She made a face. "I am getting bored. It's good you came. I can hardly wait to get out of here."

"That's good. Give it a week, and you will be out and about with me."

"How is your dad?"

"He is happy we sorted things out between us."

"Yes, that is good. And you do know that I was a really good girl? Last week, before the accident, I talked to Dr Bernstein and told him I was working only five shifts and would not pick up extra."

Then she felt embarrassed.

"But I've already told you that – sorry! I'm repeating myself!"

She was so adorable.

"Yes, I can see you're learning what you want and your priorities."

Playfully, she added, "Well, I have a very intelligent boyfriend and I do not want to lose him. Actually, I want to spend more time with him." She looked at me with her lovely blue eyes and repeated, "I want to spend more time with you and get to know you better."

"Seems great. However, I am not perfect; please remember that! You do amaze me, though. I am surprised you spoke with the doctor, knowing how much you love your job."

She spoke without hesitation.

"Jack, I do need to know my priorities. My life was work-centred, and I did not have a private life, or an independent life. Now that the Lord has given me a new direction, I want to take it. My priorities have changed, and my job no longer comes first. Yes, it provides for me and I love my job, but I want to have a life with you and see how it goes on this journey of love."

"Yes, as we are both children of God, I am sure the Lord will guide us and help us in this beautiful relationship as we walk this new journey together. In fact, I have not dated for years. When I was in my late 20s, I dated a girl for a few months, and that was it. After that, I kind of had enough of it and got bored. I was searching for someone special; then, after a while, I gave up and just dreamed and prayed."

I sat next to her on a chair and took her hand in mine.

"Then, when I met you at the hospital and you came and spent time with me and we became friends, I realised that you were the one I had been searching for."

"Let's hope you won't get bored with me."

"No, I won't Hannah. You make music to my heart." I glanced at my watch. "Listen, my angel, I have to go. I am meeting Mike tonight. Patricia asked about you, but I forgot to tell you."

I leaned over and kissed her on the cheek, and Hannah held me tight. I laughed. "You are holding me so tight! Don't worry, I am coming back tomorrow. All right, my princess."

"All right, Jack; you are in my prayers."

***

The last couple of weeks passed quickly and it was finally time to go home. Jack collected me from the hospital, and as he opened the car door, he lifted me in his arms, so happy that I was home.

"That's nice, but do you have the house keys?"

"Don't ruin the moment! I am your knight!" He was laughing.

He carried me in his arms, and Benny, so happy to see me, came rushing toward us. Jack stumbled over him and we crashed onto one of the couches.

I felt my heart beating quickly, and he slowly touched my lips and kissed me. It was so unexpected, but it felt as if it lasted a very long time.

Then we sat next to each other and were quiet. He was holding me in his arms, and Benny jumped up and curled up next to me on the couch.

"I believe it is time for me to go home. What do you think?"

"Yes, otherwise it might get too hot in here," I teased.

"I think it is getting hot already!" He laughed.

We walked to the door and Jack kissed me again, and then he left, but as he was getting into his car, he said, "Don't forget tomorrow. I won't be seeing you as I am travelling to a meeting. I will be back either tomorrow evening or the next day. I will try to call you."

Home at last and a few more days to rest. I was keen to start doing things again as I'd spent too much time lying around in hospital.

Chapter 14

Make music to my heart

It was the last Friday in November and it had been another busy day at work. I had just finished my shift and I was going home.

Jack had called me earlier and asked me to go out for dinner with him, so I had a few hours to rest and he would pick me up at 5 pm.

It was a beautiful evening, even though it was November. It had not snowed yet, and the past few days had been dry and sunny. It felt like a day in late autumn.

When I heard the doorbell, I was not quite ready. "Hi, Jack. Come in, come in!"

He was wearing a nice shirt and looked very smart.

Ecclesiastes 3:11

He has made everything beautiful in its time. Also, he has put eternity into man's heart, yet so that he cannot find out what God has done from the beginning to the end.

He looked at me and made a face.

"I can see Cinderella is not ready to go out!"

"No, I am not. I'll be ready in a minute. Say hello to Benny while I go upstairs and get dressed. Shall I put on something nice as you look amazingly handsome?"

He took me by the hand and turned me around to the music.

"Yes, please, try to find something that will make you look like a princess!"

"All right… all right."

I was in a rush and not sure what to wear. Laura was the one who always advised me on those matters. I did not have much taste in fashion. Looking in my wardrobe, I saw a beautiful blue dress and quickly put it on.

The majority of my friends would have taken an hour to dress. Jack knew by now that if I said I was getting dressed, it would be 10 minutes maximum.

I looked in the mirror, put on some nice perfume, found a beautiful red rose clip and put it in my hair on one side. It looked lovely. When I looked in the mirror, I felt like a woman, not a nurse.

As I came down the stairs, Jack came out of the lounge, stopped for a moment and smiled, admiring me. I could see in his eyes how much he loved me.

He held my hand as I came down the last few stairs.

"You look beautiful!" he said and gave me a kiss. Then he held me for a moment and I could hear his heart beating.

We went to a little Italian restaurant where we had been a few times before.

"Thank you, Hannah, for coming this evening. It will be an amazing evening."

I looked at him curiously.

"You always spoil me."

***

Hannah's life had totally changed over the past few months, as had her priorities, and the Lord was working on her character.

In a way, the Lord was slowing her down and teaching her to enjoy the new road on which she had embarked. A beautiful relationship with Jack was something unexpected but a blessing. It was challenging sometimes as Jack was learning patience and they were each on different journeys. The Lord had brought them together and they were a lovely couple. The happiest of all seemed to be Matthew.

Hannah often went to their house and cooked and spent time there in the evening, and Jack would visit her house. They got to know each other and learnt about their ups and downs and personalities. Sometimes they would clash and have a lover's quarrel, but they learned to adjust and adapt and stretch. This was an honourable relationship with the Lord at the centre, and they would never spend nights together for sex was for marriage. They were very much in love but more in love with the Lord and following His path and guidance. It was an amazing friendship that blossomed into an amazing romance.

It was not always easy, but with prayer and submission to the Lord and each other, they were on the right path.

Love was the music in their hearts. That love that was growing and maturing each day into something beautiful.

Love, a new road, was full of challenges but filled with blessings. Love was binding them together and bringing them closer to God.

They were blessed to have each other, and they had been learning to treasure and see good in each other and help each other in their weaknesses. They were in love and growing in love at the speed decided by them.

"I've talked with Mike and Patricia; they asked me to help them organise their wedding."

"Yes, Patricia asked me to be her bridesmaid, so I was asked to help too. Which I am sure you already know!"

"There's quite a lot going on for both of us in the next month or so, isn't there?"

"Well, they are getting married in January, aren't they?"

"Yes, it is a bit unusual, but well, why not? They have been dating for a few years now. Each relationship is different, isn't it?"

"Yes, it is!" She looked at him and, for a moment, went back into the past.

"I will never forget the night you came into the hospital. I was lying in my bed, as I had been in a car crash, and then, a few days later, they brought you in. It was so hard for me not to be a nurse. The Lord really tested me. And then I prayed for you, and as I prayed, I had a desire to meet you."

"And you did, didn't you?"

"Yes, when I saw you lying in bed, my heart was filled with hope, and for some reason, I kept wanting to talk to you and be there for you."

"And did you know that the first time you spoke to me, I pretended to be asleep?"

She looked surprised.

"Really?"

"Yes!" He gave her a cheeky look and laughed.

"I did not know what to say to you. You kept telling me that Jesus loved me, that the Lord was good, but I did not feel at peace at all. I was hurting. And I had this beautiful nurse telling me such lovely things."

They looked at each other and both spoke at the same time.

"One day…"

"You go first, Hannah."

"Then all those conversations we had when I finished work."

"Yes, we became friends, and the day you left was the hardest for me."

"Was it, Jack?" She stretched across and reached for his hand and he took her hand in his.

"Yes, I thought you had forgotten about me. At that point, I realised you were the one who brought hope to my heart and raised faith in me, and a new life was ahead of me. And more than that, I did not want to be just a friend; I started to fall in love with you."

Jack's eyes welled with tears. Hannah touched his face tenderly as tears rolled down her face.

"When you came and told me that you were praying and thinking of me, I felt so happy. And when you left, you told me that you would miss me."

"That was very hard for me to tell you, Jack!"

"Yes, Hannah, I am sure it was."

"Memories, hey, Jack?"

"Beautiful memories, our memories. Waiting for you to come to church, waiting to see you. Missing you and hoping you were thinking of me too. And when I asked you to come to my mum's remembrance day and on the way there you wanted to go back. I would have done anything for you. And when you told me about Jessica – you thought I had someone in my life. You were just adorable."

"That was the point at which I realised that I had started to fall in love with you, and I did not know how to deal with all my feelings for you. It was so overwhelming."

Her tears were flowing, and he stood up from the table and came to give her a hug.

"Hannah, let's not get too emotional; the evening is not over."

"Yes, yes."

They had a lovely time speaking about their friends and the project Jack was so involved in.

"Jack, I was thinking that, maybe, if you want… I could help with the project too. What do you think?"

"Are you serious, Hannah?"

"I am very serious. I might be cutting one more day and working only four days. I would like to help you."

"Oh my goodness! I can't believe it. Of course, yes, please." Then looking at her, puzzled, he added, "What do you have in mind?"

"Maybe something challenging. I would like to organise a little section where people can come for free checkups for their health! I am seeking the advice of Dr Bernstein and Dr Parson. They might be helping, as well as a few nurses. We'll see how the Lord guides."

"My dad asked me, with the team of leaders, if I wanted to preach.

What do you think, angel?"

She smiled.

"Jack, I believe you can try. Is it in your heart?"

"Yes, actually, but I am not sure that I would like to preach each Sunday."

"Then follow your heart and see what the Lord says."

It was getting late and he put his hand into his pocket.

"This is for you, my angel!"

"You spoil me, Jack!"

"You deserve it, Hannah. Without you, my life would not be so blessed. I would be alone and bored. Ha ha."

She opened the box and saw a beautiful gold necklace with a small pendant representing an angel.

"This is for you, Hannah. My angel! And it has your name on the back."

"I'm overwhelmed! Thank you, Jack."

"Do you want a hug?" he said, teasing her.

"Jack!"

On the way home, he asked her to come to his house for a cup of tea and she agreed. That night,

Matthew was not there and would be coming home late.

"I love your house, Jack, with this big, open-plan living area."

"What else would you like with your tea? A biscuit, chocolate?"

"Yes, let's have chocolate."

He picked up a big box of chocolates and sat next to her on the couch.

"It's so quiet here!"

"It has always been a quiet street and I love it. We have been here since I was 15, I think, and it is a very good neighbourhood."

Hannah leaned her head on his chest and they cuddled on the couch.

"Are you tired?"

"Not very, when I am with you. Even if I am, I forget."

Their eyes met and he smiled.

"Yes, time is something I forget too when I am with you, Hannah."

He stood up from the couch.

"Let me go into the kitchen – I forgot something else!"

"I've just got comfortable and cosy with you."

A few minutes later, he returned, looking at her with love and admiration.

"Yes, Jack Miller?" she said, waiting for a funny reply.

He went down on one knee and took her by the hand.

"Hannah Reynolds, the moment I saw you, I adored you. I love you and would like to spend the rest of my life with you. Would you do me the honour of becoming my wife?" He took a little box from his pocket and gave it to Hannah.

Speechless, she opened the box and found a beautiful blue diamond ring.

"My heart says it is the right time, and I have been praying about it, my angel." He waited, looking at her. She smiled and looked straight into his eyes as she stood up from the couch:

"Jack Miller, it is a yes. My heart says the same. And I love you. Let's go for it. Let's walk together through the challenges of life as one heart."

He took the ring and put it on her finger, with tears running down his face.

Looking deep into her eyes, he touched her face and her hair and their lips met. He kissed her passionately. Then both smiled and she leaned on his chest as he took her in his arms.

There was music in their hearts; it was love.

At that moment, the door opened and Matthew came in. Hannah and Jack did not move at all, staying silent in each other's arms.

"Oops… I'd better go to my study and have some dinner. I'll leave you two lovebirds!"

"Dad, please join us! We brought you some dinner from the Italian restaurant."

"What a thoughtful, caring son I have!" He paused. "What is going on? Am I missing something?"

Jack took Hannah's hand and put it on his chest.

"Dad, I've asked Hannah to marry me and she said yes."

"Are you crazy?" Laughing, he corrected himself. "Are you serious?"

"My heart says yes, and his heart says yes, Matthew."

"Do we have your blessing, Dad?"

Matthew felt quite overwhelmed.

"I am getting too old for surprises like this! I might have a heart attack! Ha ha."

He went up to them, took Hannah's hand and put it in Jack's hand.

"What God has joined together, no one will separate. Jack, Hannah… I am very, very happy and you have my blessing."

"We talked about getting married in March – what do you think?"

"Jack, slow down a bit! March?"

"Yes, Dad!"

"I would like you and Hannah to live here. It is a big house and, worst case scenario, we could extend it or build a bungalow for me in the garden." He laughed.

"Well, we did not think of that. But you know I love this house a lot."

"Thank you, Matthew. I would love to come and live here with Jack once we are married."

It was a beautiful evening, and the three had a lovely time talking till late.

***

When you hear music in your heart, remember it is love.
Do not quench the fire, but let it grow;
it only takes a flame and it will burn forever.

Let your love keep growing.
When there is music in your heart, it is love.
God is love.
Love is in us, through us and for us.
Open your eyes and ears, open your heart to love.
Find the right person.
You will know it is the right one
when you hear music in your heart.

The End

Bible References
English Standard Version (ESV)

Chapter 1

Matthew 11:28-30
Come to me, all who labor and are heavy laden, and I will give you rest. Take my yoke upon you, and learn from me, for I am gentle and lowly in heart, and you will find rest for your souls. For my yoke is easy, and my burden is light.

1 Peter 5:7
Casting all your anxieties on him, because he cares for you.

Psalm 16:11
You make known to me the path of life; in your presence there is fullness of joy; at your right hand are pleasures forevermore.

John 14:2
In my Father's house are many rooms. If it were not so, would I have told you that I go to prepare a place for you?

Revelation 21:4
He will wipe away every tear from their eyes, and death shall be no more, neither shall there be mourning, nor crying, nor pain anymore, for the former things have passed away.

1 Peter 2:24
He himself bore our sins in his body on the tree, that we might die to sin and live to righteousness. By his wounds you have been healed.

1 Peter 3:8
Finally, all of you, have unity of mind, sympathy, brotherly love, a tender heart, and a humble mind.

John 3:16
For God so loved the world, that he gave his only Son, that whoever believes in him should not perish but have eternal life.

Luke 6:38
Give, and it will be given to you. Good measure, pressed down, shaken together, running over, will be put into your lap. For with the measure you use it will be measured back to you.

Chapter 2

Ephesians 6:18
Praying at all times in the Spirit, with all prayer and supplication. To that end keep alert with all perseverance, making supplication for all the saints.

James 5:16

Therefore, confess your sins to one another and pray for one another, that you may be healed. The prayer of a righteous person has great power as it is working.

Isaiah 40:31

But they who wait for the LORD shall renew their strength; they shall mount up with wings like eagles; they shall run and not be weary; they shall walk and not faint.

Psalm 27:14

Wait for the Lord; be strong, and let your heart take courage; wait for the Lord!

1 Timothy 6:12

Fight the good fight of the faith. Take hold of the eternal life to which you were called and about which you made the good confession in the presence of many witnesses.

1 Corinthians 16:13

Be watchful, stand firm in the faith, act like men, be strong.

James 4:6

But he gives more grace. Therefore it says, "God opposes the proud, but gives grace to the humble."

1 Corinthians 15:10

But by the grace of God I am what I am, and his grace toward me was not in vain. On the contrary,

I worked harder than any of them, though it was not I but the grace of God that is with me.

Chapter 3

Philippians 2:4
Let each of you look not only to his own interests, but also to the interests of others.

1 Peter 2:9
But you are a chosen race, a royal priesthood, a holy nation, a people for his own possession, that you may proclaim the excellencies of him who called you out of darkness into his marvelous light.

2 Timothy 1:7
For God gave us a spirit not of fear but of power and love and self-control.

Colossians 3:12-13
Put on then, as God's chosen ones, holy and beloved, compassionate hearts, kindness, humility, meekness, and patience, bearing with one another and, if one has a complaint against another, forgiving each other; as the Lord has forgiven you, so you also must forgive.

2 Peter 3:9
The Lord is not slow to fulfill his promise as some count slowness, but is patient toward you, not wishing that any should perish, but that all should reach repentance.

Isaiah 49:16
Behold, I have engraved you on the palms of my hands; your walls are continually before me.

Mark 10:27
Jesus looked at them and said, "With man it is impossible, but not with God. For all things are possible with God."

Jeremiah 32:27
Behold, I am the Lord, the God of all flesh. Is anything too hard for me?

Chapter 4

2 Timothy 4:7
I have fought the good fight, I have finished the race, I have kept the faith.

Philippians 4:13
I can do all things through him who strengthens me.

Isaiah 43:18-19
Remember not the former things, nor consider the things of old. Behold, I am doing a new thing; now it springs forth, do you not perceive it? I will make a way in the wilderness and rivers in the desert.

Luke 9:62
Jesus said to him, "No one who puts his hand to the plow and looks back is fit for the kingdom of God."

Isaiah 41:10

Fear not, for I am with you; be not dismayed, for I am your God; I will strengthen you, I will help you, I will uphold you with my righteous right hand.

1 John 1:9

If we confess our sins, he is faithful and just to forgive us our sins and to cleanse us from all unrighteousness.

Proverbs 24:16

For the righteous falls seven times and rises again, but the wicked stumble in times of calamity.

2 Timothy 3:16-17

All Scripture is breathed out by God and profitable for teaching, for reproof, for correction, and for training in righteousness, that the man of God may be competent, equipped for every good work.

John 8:32

And you will know the truth, and the truth will set you free.

John 14:6

Jesus said to him, "I am the way, and the truth, and the life. No one comes to the Father except through me."

Psalm 90:17

Let the favor of the Lord our God be upon us and establish the work of our hands upon us; yes, establish the work of our hands!

Luke 2:52

And Jesus increased in wisdom and in stature and in favor with God and man.

Psalm 5:12

For you bless the righteous, O Lord; you cover him with favor as with a shield.

John 1:3

All things were made through him, and without him was not any thing made that was made.

Isaiah 40:31

But they who wait for the Lord shall renew their strength; they shall mount up with wings like eagles; they shall run and not be weary; they shall walk and not faint.

1 Thessalonians 5:18

Give thanks in all circumstances; for this is the will of God in Christ Jesus for you.

Ephesians 5:20-21

Giving thanks always and for everything to God the Father in the name of our Lord Jesus Christ, submitting to one another out of reverence for Christ.

Chapter 5

John 14:27

Peace I leave with you; my peace I give to you. Not as the world gives do I give to you. Let not your hearts be troubled, neither let them be afraid.

Psalm 118:5-6

Out of my distress I called on the Lord; the Lord answered me and set me free. The Lord is on my side; I will not fear. What can man do to me?

Jeremiah 1:5

Before I formed you in the womb I knew you, and before you were born I consecrated you; I appointed you a prophet to the nations.

Romans 12:12

Rejoice in hope, be patient in tribulation, be constant in prayer.

Philippians 4:4

Rejoice in the Lord always; again I will say, Rejoice.

Galatians 5:22-23

But the fruit of the Spirit is love, joy, peace, patience, kindness, goodness, faithfulness, gentleness, and self-control; against such things there is no law.

Matthew 10:33-34

But whoever denies me before men, I also will deny before my Father who is in heaven. Do not think that I have come to bring peace to the earth. I have not come to bring peace, but a sword.

Philippians 4:6-7

Do not be anxious about anything, but in everything by prayer and supplication with thanksgiving let your requests be made known to God. And the peace of God, which surpasses all understanding, will guard your hearts and your minds in Christ Jesus.

Proverbs 24:3-4
By wisdom a house is built, and by understanding it is established; by knowledge the rooms are filled with all precious and pleasant riches.

1 Corinthians 13:13
So now faith, hope, and love abide, these three; but the greatest of these is love.

John 4:24
God is spirit, and those who worship him must worship in spirit and truth.

John 1:18
No one has ever seen God; the only God, who is at the Father's side, he has made him known.

John 8:31-32
So Jesus said to the Jews who had believed in him, "If you abide in my word, you are truly my disciples, and you will know the truth, and the truth will set you free."

John 16:13
When the Spirit of truth comes, he will guide you into all the truth, for he will not speak on his own authority, but whatever he hears he will speak, and he will declare to you the things that are to come.

Ephesians 6:18-20
Praying at all times in the Spirit, with all prayer and supplication. To that end keep alert with all perseverance, making supplication for all the saints, and also for me, that words may be given to me in opening my mouth boldly to proclaim the mystery of the gospel, for which I am an ambassador in chains, that I may declare it boldly, as I ought to speak.

Chapter 6

Proverbs 16:3
Commit your work to the Lord, and your plans will be established.

1 Corinthians 10:31
So, whether you eat or drink, or whatever you do, do all to the glory of God.

Luke 1:37
For nothing will be impossible with God.

Ephesians 2:10
For we are his workmanship, created in Christ Jesus for good works, which God prepared beforehand, that we should walk in them.

Proverbs 4:23
Keep your heart with all vigilance, for from it flow the springs of life.

Psalm 20:4-6

May he grant you your heart's desire and fulfill all your plans! May we shout for joy over your salvation, and in the name of our God set up our banners! May the LORD fulfill all your petitions! Now I know that the LORD saves his anointed; he will answer him from his holy heaven with the saving might of his right hand.

Proverbs 15:13

A glad heart makes a cheerful face, but by sorrow of heart the spirit is crushed.

Chapter 7

Proverbs 14:1

The wisest of women builds her house, but folly with her own hands tears it down.

John 3:6

That which is born of the flesh is flesh, and that which is born of the Spirit is spirit.

John 17:4

I glorified you on earth, having accomplished the work that you gave me to do.

Isaiah 53:4-5

Surely he has borne our griefs and carried our sorrows; yet we esteemed him stricken, smitten by God, and afflicted. But he was wounded for our transgressions; he was crushed for our iniquities; upon him was the chastisement that brought us peace, and with his stripes we are healed.

Romans 11:6
But if it is by grace, it is no longer on the basis of works; otherwise grace would no longer be grace.

Romans 3:24-25
And are justified by his grace as a gift, through the redemption that is in Christ Jesus, whom God put forward as a propitiation by his blood, to be received by faith. This was to show God's righteousness, because in his divine forbearance he had passed over former sins.

Isaiah 43:2
When you pass through the waters, I will be with you; and through the rivers, they shall not overwhelm you; when you walk through fire you shall not be burned, and the flame shall not consume you.

Matthew 5:6-8
Blessed are those who hunger and thirst for righteousness, for they shall be satisfied. Blessed are the merciful, for they shall receive mercy. Blessed are the pure in heart, for they shall see God.

Psalm 56:8
You have kept count of my tossings; put my tears in your bottle. Are they not in your book?

Psalm 126:5

Those who sow in tears shall reap with shouts of joy!

Proverbs 18:22

He who finds a wife finds a good thing and obtains favor from the Lord.

Psalm 90:17

Let the favor of the Lord our God be upon us, and establish the work of our hands upon us; yes, establish the work of our hands!

Psalm 5:12

For you bless the righteous, O Lord; you cover him with favor as with a shield.

Chapter 8

John 10:27

My sheep hear my voice, and I know them, and they follow me.

Psalm 111:10

The fear of the Lord is the beginning of wisdom; all those who practice it have a good understanding. His praise endures forever!

Proverbs 30:5-6

Every word of God proves true; he is a shield to those who take refuge in him. Do not add to his words, lest he rebuke you and you be found a liar.

John 15:13

Greater love has no one than this, that someone lay down his life for his friends.

Proverbs 17:17

A friend loves at all times, and a brother is born for adversity.

Proverbs 27:17

Iron sharpens iron, and one man sharpens another.

Psalm 37:4-6

Delight yourself in the Lord, and he will give you the desires of your heart. Commit your way to the Lord; trust in him, and he will act. He will bring forth your righteousness as the light, and your justice as the noonday.

Romans 8:26

Likewise the Spirit helps us in our weakness. For we do not know what to pray for as we ought, but the Spirit himself intercedes for us with groanings too deep for words.

Colossians 3:14-17

And above all these put on love, which binds everything together in perfect harmony. And let the peace of Christ rule in your hearts, to which indeed you were called in one body. And be thankful. Let the word of Christ dwell in you richly, teaching and admonishing one another in all wisdom, singing psalms and hymns and spiritual songs, with thankfulness in your hearts to God. And whatever you do, in word or deed, do everything in the name of the Lord Jesus, giving thanks to God the Father through him.

Chapter 9

1 Peter 2:5
You yourselves like living stones are being built up as a spiritual house, to be a holy priesthood, to offer spiritual sacrifices acceptable to God through Jesus Christ.

1 Corinthians 6:19-20
Or do you not know that your body is a temple of the Holy Spirit within you, whom you have from God? You are not your own, for you were bought with a price. So glorify God in your body.

Ephesians 2:8
For by grace you have been saved through faith. And this is not your own doing; it is the gift of God,

James 1:12
Blessed is the man who remains steadfast under trial, for when he has stood the test he will receive the crown of life, which God has promised to those who love him.

Hebrews 10:36

For you have need of endurance, so that when you have done the will of God you may receive what is promised.

Psalm 34:17-20

When the righteous cry for help, the Lord hears and delivers them out of all their troubles. The Lord is near to the brokenhearted and saves the crushed in spirit. Many are the afflictions of the righteous, but the Lord delivers him out of them all. He keeps all his bones; not one of them is broken.

2 Corinthians 12:9

But he said to me, "My grace is sufficient for you, for my power is made perfect in weakness." Therefore I will boast all the more gladly of my weaknesses, so that the power of Christ may rest upon me.

Psalm 119:169

Let my cry come before you, O Lord; give me understanding according to your word!

John 14:26

But the Helper, the Holy Spirit, whom the Father will send in my name, he will teach you all things and bring to your remembrance all that I have said to you.

Ephesians 4:26-28

Be angry and do not sin; do not let the sun go down on your anger, and give no opportunity to the devil.

Let the thief no longer steal, but rather let him labor, doing honest work with his own hands, so that he may have something to share with anyone in need.

Proverbs 15:1
A soft answer turns away wrath, but a harsh word stirs up anger.

Chapter 10

Matthew 22:37-39
And he said to him, "You shall love the Lord your God with all your heart and with all your soul and with all your mind. This is the great and first commandment. And a second is like it: You shall love your neighbor as yourself."

Philippians 2:9-11
Therefore God has highly exalted him and bestowed on him the name that is above every name, so that at the name of Jesus every knee should bow, in heaven and on earth and under the earth, and every tongue confess that Jesus Christ is Lord, to the glory of God the Father.

Proverbs 15:13-14
A glad heart makes a cheerful face, but by sorrow of heart the spirit is crushed. The heart of him who has understanding seeks knowledge, but the mouths of fools feed on folly.

Psalm 119:135
Make your face shine upon your servant, and teach me your statutes.

Psalm 23:1-6
A Psalm of David. The LORD is my shepherd; I shall not want. He makes me lie down in green pastures. He leads me beside still waters. He restores my soul. He leads me in paths of righteousness for his name's sake. Even though I walk through the valley of the shadow of death, I will fear no evil, for you are with me; your rod and your staff, they comfort me. You prepare a table before me in the presence of my enemies; you anoint my head with oil; my cup overflows.

Hebrew 13:8
Jesus Christ is the same yesterday and today and forever.

1 John 4:6-8
We are from God. Whoever knows God listens to us; whoever is not from God does not listen to us. By this we know the Spirit of truth and the spirit of error. Beloved, let us love one another, for love is from God, and whoever loves has been born of God and knows God. Anyone who does not love does not know God, because God is love.

Proverbs 10:12
Hatred stirs up strife, but love covers all offenses.

1 John 4:19

We love because he first loved us.

Chapter 11

Matthew 7:13-14

Enter by the narrow gate. For the gate is wide and the way is easy that leads to destruction, and those who enter by it are many. For the gate is narrow and the way is hard that leads to life, and those who find it are few.

John 6:37-39

All that the Father gives me will come to me, and whoever comes to me I will never cast out. For I have come down from heaven, not to do my own will but the will of him who sent me. And this is the will of him who sent me, that I should lose nothing of all that he has given me, but raise it up on the last day.

John 1:12-14

But to all who did receive him, who believed in his name, he gave the right to become children of God, who were born, not of blood nor of the will of the flesh nor of the will of man, but of God. And the Word became flesh and dwelt among us, and we have seen his glory, glory as of the only Son from the Father, full of grace and truth.

Romans 10:13

For "everyone who calls on the name of the Lord will be saved."

Revelation 3:20

Behold, I stand at the door and knock. If anyone hears my voice and opens the door, I will come in to him and eat with him, and he with me.

Luke 16:13

No servant can serve two masters, for either he will hate the one and love the other, or he will be devoted to the one and despise the other. You cannot serve God and money.

1 Timothy 2:1-2

I urge, then, first of all, that petitions, prayers, intercession and thanksgiving be made for all people, for kings and all those in authority, that we may live peaceful and quiet lives in all godliness and holiness.

Philippians 4:8-9

Finally, brothers, whatever is true, whatever is honorable, whatever is just, whatever is pure, whatever is lovely, whatever is commendable, if there is any excellence, if there is anything worthy of praise, think about these things. What you have learned and received and heard and seen in me—practice these things, and the God of peace will be with you.

Matthew 6:14-15

For if you forgive others their trespasses, your heavenly Father will also forgive you, but if you do

not forgive others their trespasses, neither will your
Father forgive your trespasses.

Romans 8:5-6
For those who live according to the flesh set their
minds on the things of the flesh, but those who live
according to the Spirit set their minds on the things
of the Spirit. For to set the mind on the flesh is death,
but to set the mind on the Spirit is life and peace.

2 Corinthians 10:5-6
We destroy arguments and every lofty opinion raised
against the knowledge of God, and take every thought
captive to obey Christ, being ready to punish every
disobedience, when your obedience is complete.

Isaiah 26:3
You keep him in perfect peace whose mind is stayed
on you, because he trusts in you.

Chapter 12

Hebrews 4:12
For the word of God is living and active, sharper
than any two-edged sword, piercing to the division
of soul and of spirit, of joints and of marrow, and
discerning the thoughts and intentions of the heart.

Romans 12:1-2
I appeal to you therefore, brothers, by the mercies
of God, to present your bodies as a living sacrifice,

holy and acceptable to God, which is your spiritual worship. Do not be conformed to this world, but be transformed by the renewal of your mind, that by testing you may discern what is the will of God, what is good and acceptable and perfect.

Matthew 7:1-2
Judge not, that you be not judged. For with the judgment you pronounce you will be judged, and with the measure you use it will be measured to you.

James 5:20
Let him know that whoever brings back a sinner from his wandering will save his soul from death and will cover a multitude of sins.

Psalm 56:3-4
When I am afraid, I put my trust in you. In God, whose word I praise, in God I trust; I shall not be afraid. What can flesh do to me?

Proverbs 3:5-6
Trust in the LORD with all your heart, and do not lean on your own understanding. In all your ways acknowledge him, and he will make straight your paths.

Isaiah 26:3-4
You keep him in perfect peace whose mind is stayed on you, because he trusts in you. Trust in the Lord forever, for the Lord God is an everlasting rock.

Psalm 13:5

But I have trusted in your steadfast love; my heart shall rejoice in your salvation.

Psalm 55:22

Cast your burden on the Lord, and he will sustain you; he will never permit the righteous to be moved.

Philippians 1:6

And I am sure of this, that he who began a good work in you will bring it to completion at the day of Jesus Christ.

Galatians 6:2

Bear one another's burdens, and so fulfill the law of Christ.

Chapter 13

Matthew 17:20

He said to them, "Because of your little faith. For truly, I say to you, if you have faith like a grain of mustard seed, you will say to this mountain, 'Move from here to there,' and it will move, and nothing will be impossible for you."

John 14:12-15

Truly, truly, I say to you, whoever believes in me will also do the works that I do; and greater works than these will he do, because I am going to the Father. Whatever you ask in my name, this I will do, that the Father may be glorified in the Son. If you ask me anything in my name, I will do it. If you love me, you will keep my commandments.

Psalm 77:14
You are the God who works wonders; you have made known your might among the peoples.

Psalm 33:11
The counsel of the Lord stands forever, the plans of his heart to all generations.

Proverbs 19:21
Many are the plans in the mind of a man, but it is the purpose of the Lord that will stand.

1 John 4:16
So we have come to know and to believe the love that God has for us. God is love, and whoever abides in love abides in God, and God abides in him.

1 Corinthians 2:9-11
But, as it is written, "What no eye has seen, nor ear heard, nor the heart of man imagined, what God has prepared for those who love him"— these things God has revealed to us through the Spirit. For the Spirit searches everything, even the depths of God. For who knows a person's thoughts except the spirit of that person, which is in him? So also no one comprehends the thoughts of God except the Spirit of God.

1 Peter 5:6-7

Humble yourselves, therefore, under the mighty hand of God so that at the proper time he may exalt you, casting all your anxieties on him, because he cares for you.

Ephesians 4:15-16

Rather, speaking the truth in love, we are to grow up in every way into him who is the head, into Christ, from whom the whole body, joined and held together by every joint with which it is equipped, when each part is working properly, makes the body grow so that it builds itself up in love.

James 1:19-20

Know this, my beloved brothers: let every person be quick to hear, slow to speak, slow to anger; for the anger of man does not produce the righteousness of God.

Colossians 4:6

Let your speech always be gracious, seasoned with salt, so that you may know how you ought to answer each person.

Psalm 19:14

Let the words of my mouth and the meditation of my heart be acceptable in your sight, O Lord, my rock and my redeemer.

Psalm 91:1-2

He who dwells in the shelter of the Most High will abide in the shadow of the Almighty. I will say to the Lord, "My refuge and my fortress, my God, in whom I trust."

Jeremiah 29:11-13

For I know the plans I have for you, declares the LORD, plans for welfare and not for evil, to give you a future and a hope. Then you will call upon me and come and pray to me, and I will hear you. You will seek me and find me, when you seek me with all your heart.

Joshua 24:15

And if it is evil in your eyes to serve the Lord, choose this day whom you will serve, whether the gods your fathers served in the region beyond the River, or the gods of the Amorites in whose land you dwell. But as for me and my house, we will serve the Lord.

Chapter 14

Ecclesiastes 3:11

He has made everything beautiful in its time. Also, he has put eternity into man's heart, yet so that he cannot find out what God has done from the beginning to the end.

James 1:17

Every good gift and every perfect gift is from above, coming down from the Father of lights with whom there is no variation or shadow due to change.

2 Corinthians 9:8

And God is able to make all grace abound to you, so that having all sufficiency in all things at all times, you may abound in every good work.

Philippians 2:13

For it is God who works in you, both to will and to work for his good pleasure.

Matthew 6:33

But seek first the kingdom of God and his righteousness, and all these things will be added to you.

John 13:34-35

A new commandment I give to you, that you love one another: just as I have loved you, you also are to love one another. By this all people will know that you are my disciples, if you have love for one another.

Romans 5:8

But God shows his love for us in that while we were still sinners, Christ died for us.

Ephesians 2:4-7

But God, being rich in mercy, because of the great love with which he loved us, even when we were dead in our trespasses, made us alive together with Christ—by grace you have been saved— and raised us up with him and seated us with him in the heavenly places in Christ Jesus, so that in the coming ages he might show the immeasurable riches of his grace in kindness toward us in Christ Jesus.

1 John 4:10

In this is love, not that we have loved God but that he loved us and sent his Son to be the propitiation for our sins.

1 Corinthians 13:4-7

Love is patient and kind; love does not envy or boast; it is not arrogant or rude. It does not insist on its own way; it is not irritable or resentful; it does not rejoice at wrongdoing, but rejoices with the truth. Love bears all things, believes all things, hopes all things, endures all things.

Jon 15:13

Greater love has no one than this, that someone lay down his life for his friends.

Genesis 2:24

Therefore a man shall leave his father and his mother and hold fast to his wife, and they shall become one flesh.

"The Boundaries of my Heart", by Grace True is a Christian novel that has a beautiful story that talks about how the Lord works in our lives, a love story that starts with friendship and leads to a beautiful relationship guided by the Lord.

The most important thing was to invite the Lord into the situation and ask Him for wisdom. I loved sitting at Jesus' feet and listening. The Lord always revealed things to me and showed me ways that would never have crossed my mind.

His ways are higher than our ways. His will and timing are the best. Patience and perseverance in waiting on the Lord are key to taking the right steps, making the right choices.

The Lord is near to us in every circumstance and fire we go through. We just need to call upon His name, and His Spirit will lead us and comfort us.

Printed in Great Britain
by Amazon